		DATE DUE	

How Does Fake News Threaten Society?

John Allen

ReferencePoint
Press®

San Diego, CA

ReferencePoint
Press®

About the Author

John Allen is a writer who lives in Oklahoma City.

© 2021 ReferencePoint Press, Inc.
Printed in the United States

For more information, contact:
ReferencePoint Press, Inc.
PO Box 27779
San Diego, CA 92198
www.ReferencePointPress.com

LIBRARY OF CONGRESS CATALOGING-IN-PUBLICATION DATA

Names: Allen, John, 1957- author.
Title: How does fake news threaten society? / by John Allen.
Description: San Diego : ReferencePoint Press, 2020. | Series: Issues today
   | Includes bibliographical references and index.
Identifiers: LCCN 2019053954 (print) | LCCN 2019053955 (ebook) | ISBN
   9781682828793 (library binding) | ISBN 9781682828809 (ebook)
Subjects: LCSH: Fake news--Social aspects--Juvenile literature. |
   Disinformation--Juvenile literature.
Classification: LCC PN4784.F27 A45 2020 (print) | LCC PN4784.F27 (ebook)
   | DDC 070.4/3--dc23
LC record available at https://lccn.loc.gov/2019053954
LC ebook record available at https://lccn.loc.gov/2019053955

Trolling the Public

Reports surfaced online in 2018 that an Illinois man who had won millions in the lottery spent $224,000 of it to dump tons of manure on his ex-boss's front yard. First published on a site called World News Daily Report, the story went viral on Facebook. It garnered nearly 2.4 million shares, reactions, and comments. The story was funny—satisfying even—and completely untrue. According to data sites BuzzSumo and Trendolizer, the lottery dumper tale was the number one fake news story on Facebook in 2018. In fact, the top fifty fake stories generated about 22 million shares and comments. That is a lot of manure. Nonetheless, Facebook officials say the overall amount of fake news on its platform is going down. "We've been working hard to stop the spread of false news on Facebook, and we're encouraged by the results," says Tessa Lyons, a Facebook product manager who oversees the company's anti-misinformation efforts. "Still, we know this is a highly adversarial issue and takes a multi-pronged approach."[1]

The Spread of Fake News

The story of the lottery dumper is a prime example of fake news. Such stories are often meant to be so-called clickbait, enticing readers to click on a link to read more. Fake news may focus on celebrities, political figures, athletes, and other people in the public eye. Some fake news is made up of quirky stories intended for entertainment. For example, the tale about the Illinois lottery winner appeared on a satirical website. A disclaimer on the site explains that its content is wholly invented, but many readers might not notice this detail. "I guess it is humor to a certain extent, but people need to read to the bottom and find out it's not a real news story," says Len Austin, head of the village

4

in Illinois where the dumping was supposed to have happened. "The problem these days is that people see a headline online and jump to conclusions."[2]

Other fake news has a more sinister purpose. It seeks to stir up anger, sow distrust, and destroy reputations. False stories may accuse government officials of unethical or illegal behavior, such as taking bribes or peddling influence. Political candidates can be linked to extremist views they have never endorsed. Public figures may be falsely quoted as making inflammatory remarks. Businesses can face boycotts or backlash due to false or exaggerated claims. When fake news is shared on social media such as Facebook, Twitter, Instagram, and YouTube, many users assume it is true.

A Loss of Trust

In fact, today's social media and communication technology enable fake news to spread more quickly than ever before. False stories go viral on a million smartphones before legitimate news organizations and fact-checking sites can debunk them. Millions of bots, or software robots, spread fake news on social media platforms using artificial intelligence. Trolls, or mischief makers on social media, plant made-up stories, attack the credibility of ideas they oppose, and try to bully other users. Their efforts to promote lies and distortions are called trolling. Whether intentionally or not, many people on social media pass along false stories to their Facebook groups or Twitter followers. The result is a constant circulation of fake news.

President Donald Trump adds to the confusion over what is true. Trump frequently labels the national media as fake news. Shortly after taking office, he blasted the media in a notorious tweet: "The FAKE NEWS media (failing @nytimes, @CNN, @NBCNews and many more) is not my enemy, it is the enemy of the American people. SICK!"[3] At the same time, Trump promotes his own dubious claims in speeches and numerous tweets.

In such an atmosphere, people can grow skeptical about virtually all news stories. A Gallup poll released in September 2019 showed that only 13 percent of Americans have a great deal of trust in the news media, while only 28 percent have even a fair amount of trust. Analysts say the gradual loss of trust in the media is a threat to a healthy democracy. "In order for the media to play its role as a watchdog, it relies on public trust," says James Bikales, editorial writer at the *Harvard Political Review*. "The people must believe the press in order to take action based upon its reporting. Trump's rhetoric on the media has undermined this trust, threatening the nation's democratic system."[4]

> "In order for the media to play its role as a watchdog, it relies on public trust. The people must believe the press in order to take action based upon its reporting."[4]
>
> —James Bikales, editorial writer at the *Harvard Political Review*

The widespread use of social media and smartphone technology enables fake news to spread more widely and quickly than ever before. False stories go viral well before legitimate news organizations and fact-checking sites can debunk them.

Combating Fake News

The torrent of fake news today affects daily life in countless ways. And it is not only stories about politics and entertainment that are suspect. Fake news also taints public information about health care, personal health, the environment, race relations, education, stocks, and many other subjects. Readers looking for the truth can find themselves confronted by funhouse mirrors of deception and lies. Some people, including media-savvy teens, cling to a few trusted news sources and tune out nearly everything else.

Social media companies face mounting pressure to combat fake news on their platforms. Yet at the same time, they are charged with protecting free speech, even when the speech is deceptive. Some use fact-checkers to weed out false news stories. Increasingly, social media firms share information about users who purvey fake news. They are also instituting stricter guidelines on advertisements. New sensors, using artificial intelligence, show promise in identifying and eliminating fake news. Experts say the threat to public discourse demands more action. "To use a metaphor that's often used in boxing, truth is against the ropes," says Sam Wineburg, an education professor at Stanford University. "It is getting pummeled."[5]

"To use a metaphor that's often used in boxing, truth is against the ropes. It is getting pummeled."[5]

—Sam Wineburg, education professor at Stanford University

CHAPTER ONE

How Fake News Goes Viral

People are always searching for health foods that will give them energy, help them lose weight, or even stave off illness. In 2018 many turned to the latest superfood: celery juice. Thousands of enthusiasts took part in the celery juice challenge. They began to drink a 16-ounce (454 g) glass of the liquid on an empty stomach every morning for a week. In 2019 the hashtag #celeryjuicechallenge trended for months on Instagram. Trim young women posted Instagram selfies with pitchers of the bright-green juice, while users touted its miraculous properties on Twitter and Facebook.

The celery juice craze began with a best-selling author named Anthony William, who calls himself "the Medical Medium." A medium is a person who claims the ability to contact the spirit world. In keeping with that definition, William says he is aided by a spirit from the future. Celebrities from Gwyneth Paltrow to Sylvester Stallone were among his early followers. As the story spread, groceries and health food stores across the country could not keep enough celery in stock. Users claimed celery juice would remove toxins from the liver, ease the digestive system, help with rapid weight loss, and even guard against cancer. In the midst of all this chatter, medical experts tried to set the record straight. Celery juice, they observed, is no miracle drink. "There is no evidence that drinking celery juice, or any juice, has any detoxing or cleansing benefits," says Lindsay Krasna, a registered dietitian in Brooklyn, New York. "Our kidneys and liver are the vital organs responsible for purifying our blood and ridding our bodies of harmful toxins. They do that beautifully whether we're consuming celery juice or eating a burger."[6]

Social Media and Fake News

A fake news phenomenon like the celery juice challenge owes much of its rapid spread to social media. In the past few years social media sites, including Facebook, Twitter, Instagram, and YouTube, have become a vital part of people's daily lives. Many people become anxious if they do not check their smartphones every few minutes. The raw numbers of social media growth are astounding. In 2010 the number of people using social media worldwide was just under 1 billion. By 2019 that number had nearly tripled to 2.82 billion and is expected to top 3 billion by 2021. And people are spending an increasing amount of time on these platforms. According to the data site Statista, users in 2019 were projected to spend an average of 153 minutes each day on social media, or more than 2½ hours. Among the posts, photos, and links that users share, a lot of fake news gets passed around.

A closer look at William and the celery juice fad shows how social media provides the launching pad for fake news and dubious claims. William is what is known on social media as an influencer.

In 2018 and 2019, the so-called celery juice challenge went viral on social media. Adherents touted the drink's supposed miraculous health benefits, even though medical experts insisted the claims were not supported by science.

Millions of people look to him for tips on wellness, nutrition, and treatments for illness. He boasts more than 2 million followers on Instagram and 3.4 million on Facebook. William's website includes a disclaimer that he is *not* a licensed medical professional. Yet in social media posts he has declared that celery can help cure fibromyalgia, a disorder marked by muscular and skeletal pain. He has also promoted the ability of celery juice to fight cancer and diabetes. In one of his videos, William says, "I can give you clarity on diseases that doctors often misdiagnose or treat incorrectly, or they just give up on and label mystery illness."[7] Doctors reject these claims outright. Many fear that vulnerable social media users will turn to celery juice or some other

Satire: Fake News for Laughs

Some outlets produce fake news stories not to deceive people but to make a satirical point. This follows the tradition of shows like *Saturday Night Live* and its satirical news report called Weekend Update. One of the most popular websites for humorous fake news is the Onion. Billing itself as "America's Finest News Source," the Onion posts fake news stories and videos on politics, sports, and entertainment. For example, on October 24, 2019, with the House impeachment inquiry in the news, the website published a story with the fanciful headline "Trump Ties Thousands of Balloons to White House Roof in Attempt to Sail Away from Impeachment Inquiry."

Staffers at the Onion admit that the depth of the current political divide makes their task more difficult. "We're so divided in this country politically right now that I feel like people can be very dismissive if they think you're doing a joke that's critical of Trump," says editor in chief Chad Nackers. "On the other hand, I think overly left-leaning people can be too on board with anything someone says, not even an Onion thing. They'll believe anything as long as it's hammering Trump."

The Onion's success has led to imitators, like the Babylon Bee, a satirical fake news site with a conservative slant. The Bee's stories are frequently shared on social media as if they were genuine. Dozens of them have even been fact-checked by the liberal site Snopes—certainly a triumph for a writer of fake news.

Quoted in Andrew Restuccia, "How Trump Changed Everything for the Onion," *Politico*, May 21, 2018. www.politico.eu.

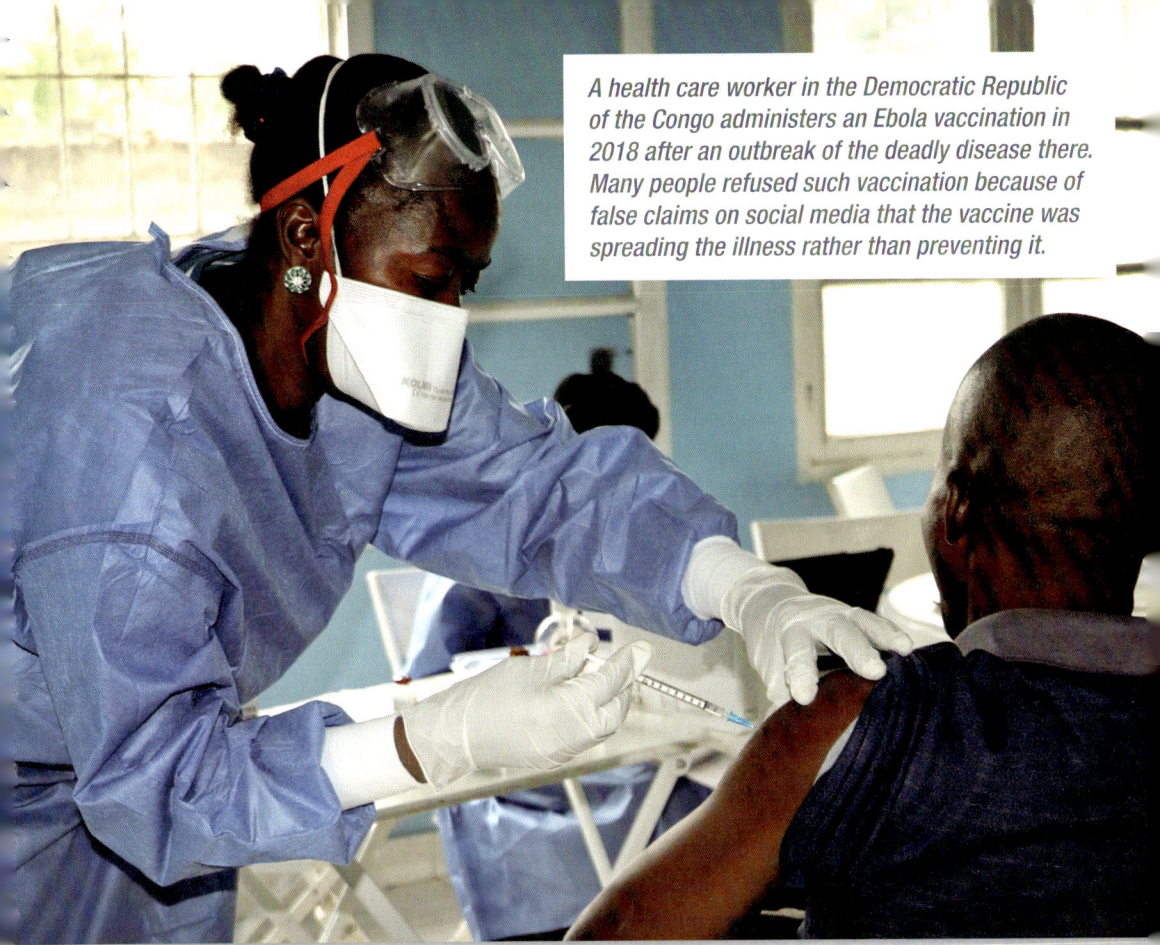

A health care worker in the Democratic Republic of the Congo administers an Ebola vaccination in 2018 after an outbreak of the deadly disease there. Many people refused such vaccination because of false claims on social media that the vaccine was spreading the illness rather than preventing it.

so-called miracle cure when they should instead be seeking professional medical care to treat an illness.

Social media's global reach has forced many countries to address the issue of fake news. In August 2018 the Democratic Republic of the Congo (DRC) in Central Africa saw an outbreak of Ebola, a deadly disease marked by high fever and severe internal bleeding. The Ebola virus is spread by contact with infected bodily fluids, so rapid quarantine is vital in order to save lives. By September 2019 about three thousand cases of Ebola had been confirmed among the Congolese, with more than two thousand proving fatal. Yet fake news and rumors shared by Twitter users in the DRC made aid workers' jobs more difficult. Word spread on social media that the experimental vaccines at health clinics were actually part of a plot to infect people with the disease. Social media also repeated false claims from a radio interview by a Congolese politician opposed to the current regime. The politician declared that the Ebola virus had been manufactured in government labs to wipe out entire cities. International health groups scrambled to get the real story out so the Congolese would go to the clinics for treatment. "I usually tell my teams that we fight two outbreaks, Ebola and fear," says Carlos Navarro Colorado of the United Nations International Children's Emergency Fund in New York City. "It is all about information."[8]

Random News Stories and Clickbait

Whereas people once got their news from a few trusted sources, they now gather stories from all corners of the internet. Today more than 60 percent of Americans acquire news from sources like Facebook's News Feed instead of a news-gathering organization like the *New York Times* or *Wall Street Journal*. What is trending on Twitter—from political news to sports stories to puff pieces on Hollywood celebrities—is often a better guide to what people are actually talking about than the evening network news reports. And amid each random menu of stories, with no news editor to make judgments on credibility, a certain amount of fake news and misleading reports generally appears.

Throughout the internet, competition for eyeballs is fierce. Since each click means advertising revenue, certain websites employ less scrupulous means of drawing attention. A frequent strategy is to lure readers with sensational or misleading headlines, called clickbait. The headline teases visitors to click on a link that takes them to a targeted web page where the complete article is located. Like a movie cliffhanger, the clickbait headline makes a visitor want to find out the rest of the story, as in "A Man Tried to Hug a Grizzly Bear and You Won't Believe What Happened Next!" Clickbait headlines also tend to use terms like *jaw-dropping* or *mind-blowing* to lure readers. Another approach is the list, such as "Seven Ways That Cyber Thieves Are Stealing Your Identity." The list requires the user to click forward to each numbered section, with a new advertisement on each page. Ultimately, clickbait articles are fake news because they deliver much

Spreading Fake News with Microtargeting

To find the most receptive audience for their misinformation, fake news websites use microtargeting. This is done with the help of cookies, which are files that websites install on a person's computer. A website makes use of cookies to store its users' preferences for reading, searching, and shopping. Once a cookie has been installed, a user's browser has been stamped with a unique ID. Some cookies, called trackers, actually track a user's activity all over the web, including all the websites visited.

Companies such as Facebook and Google use trackers to create a record of a person's web history in order to target ads to that person—that is, to personalize their marketing. That is why when someone is searching for a used car online, a number of used car ads start appearing on whatever site he or she visits. Media analytics firms use this data about a person's web usage, preferences, and "likes" to advertise everything from shoes to political candidates. But trackers can also be used to target individuals who are most likely to respond to certain fake political stories. Experts warned that microtargeting would be employed in the 2020 presidential campaign to spread false or misleading information, especially to voters in swing states. They urged people to be aware of the dangers of microtargeting. According to cyberspecialist Dipayan Ghosh, "It is thus squarely on our shoulders—as consumers, citizens, and voters—to understand the media's regime current nature and take care to protect ourselves from its rough edges."

Dipayan Ghosh, "What Is Microtargeting and What Is It Doing in Our Politics?," *Internet Citizen* (blog), Mozilla, October 4, 2018. https://blog.mozilla.org.

less than they promise. Nearly 40 percent of headlines from fake news sites resort to the clickbait style.

Clickbait headlines have become so successful at attracting readers that mainstream sites are adopting the practice. A 2017 study by researchers from the University of Mississippi and the University of Oklahoma analyzed 1.67 million Facebook posts made by 153 media organizations. The researchers found that one-third of the headlines created by the mainstream media—the print and broadcast media that are most widely circulated—used clickbait techniques. These included questions, lists, and sensational language. The clickbait headlines by mainstream media mostly included politics, entertainment, or lifestyle stories.

Fake News Websites

Fake news also is spread via websites designed to look like legitimate news sources. These fake news websites produce stories based on false information, misleading claims, or outright hoaxes. Their owners create the websites by purchasing a unique domain name and a web host, both of which can be obtained for little expense. They try to fool readers by mimicking mainstream news sites, such as one with a logo almost identical to ABC News. A site called the Boston Tribune sports a name like a legitimate newspaper and divides its dubious stories into separate departments like a major daily. The right-wing site Infowars, linked to radio host Alex Jones, employs videos and sleek graphics to promote fake news and conspiracy theories. World News Daily Report, whose fake news stories on religious and scientific topics have often gone viral, boasts that it has "news you can trust!"[9] But its site also features a disclaimer saying it is not responsible for information that happens to be incorrect. The website Huzlers attracts traffic with fake stories about disgusting health violations at national restaurant chains. A typical Huzlers story falsely claimed that a national Mexican food chain used cat and dog meat in its dishes.

Fake news websites tend to have a slippery relationship with the truth, mixing some factual content with material ranging from distortions to outright lies. Those with a political slant produce biased takes based on current issues in the news. Some sites, however, present stories that go viral simply because they are so outrageous. A good example is a headline from the News Examiner: "World's First Head Transplant a Success After Nineteen Hour Operation." And then there are satirical news websites, such as the Onion, that publish fake stories for laughs.

Technical Tricks to Fool Readers

Fake news websites also use technical tricks to fool readers, according to a recent study by DomainTools, an internet security research service. One technique is called typosquatting. It targets users who make a mistake when typing a website address into their web browser—such as www.nyytimes.com for www.nytimes.com. This ploy, also called URL hijacking, leads the user to an alternate website that may contain fake news or advertisements. Spoofing is when a publisher sends out a link via email that when clicked, sends the reader to a fake news website. A spoofing attack can also infiltrate the user's computer with malware.

According to DomainTools, these types of attacks are growing more frequent. "It's no secret that disinformation campaigns have been on the rise," says Corin Imai, a senior security advisor at DomainTools. "With the uptick in fake news sites in recent years, we were curious about the possible connection between typosquatting campaigns and the dissemination of disinformation. What we found is that domain names of top news outlets have indeed been spoofed, and subject to typosquatting techniques."[10] According to the DomainTools study, the *New York Times* has been spoofed over the years with forty-nine fake domains, the *Washington Post* with twenty, and the *New York Post* with sixteen. Fake news spoofers and scammers target news websites with the highest readership. They also set up websites on internet domains that were once valid but are now out of use.

"With the uptick in fake news sites in recent years, we were curious about the possible connection between typosquatting campaigns and the dissemination of disinformation."[10]

—Corin Imai, senior security advisor at DomainTools

Using Bots to Spread Fake News

Technology also helps spread fake news stories as effectively as actual humans. This is done by means of bots—short for *robots*. Bots are automated social media accounts that appear on platforms such as Facebook, Twitter, and Instagram. A 2017 study estimated there were 140 million bots on Facebook, 23 million on Twitter, and 27 million on Instagram. For Twitter and Instagram, this represented more than 8 percent of each platform's accounts. Bots are programmed by computer specialists to perform certain tasks over and over automatically. On a social network like Twitter, they simulate human users by interacting with other users and sharing information and messages. Through repetition, they use artificial intelligence to learn how to respond to various situations like human users do on the platform.

Bots spread misinformation in two ways. First, they post or tweet fake news items continually, and then they reply to comments or posts made by real users with the same fake items. By circulating fake news stories widely, bots are able to convince ordinary users that the stories are credible. These tactics are successful because users generally do not question too closely what is posted or shared on social media.

Social media companies have taken steps to prevent bots from spreading fake news. In July 2018 Twitter removed tens of millions of bot accounts from its platform. The effort lowered the total number of followers on Twitter by nearly 6 percent, showing the penetration of bots. In April 2019 Twitter wiped out a further five thousand bot accounts that all claimed Special Counsel Robert Mueller's investigation of Russian interference in the 2016 presidential election was a hoax. As a spokesperson for Twitter explained, "We suspended a network of accounts and others associated with it for engaging in platform manipulation—a violation of the Twitter Rules."[11]

"We suspended a network of [bot] accounts and others associated with it for engaging in platform manipulation—a violation of the Twitter Rules."[11]

—Spokesperson for Twitter

Social Media Trolls

Alongside bots, actual humans called trolls also work overtime to spread fake news and disinformation on social media. Trolls are individuals with a social media account who share fake news and attack other users in posts and comments. Trolls argue in support of fake news stories that align with their political views. They relentlessly insult users who disagree with them and try to intimidate opinion groups with name-calling and nasty comebacks. They try to inflame racial tensions and social unrest. They also attempt to undermine the credibility of genuine news stories. Trolls consider it a success when their inflammatory comments cause other users to respond with their own abusive language.

The Russian Internet Research Agency (IRA) employed agents as trolls on US social media to sow discord and disinformation in the run-up to the 2016 election. Domestic trolls exist as well, with some spreading fake news about businesses or stocks. However, since the trolls' activity is not technically illegal, they have yet to be investigated, and the extent of their activities is still in question. Platforms such as Facebook and Twitter are searching for ways to identify and eliminate troll accounts but so far have had limited success. According to Roman Sannikov, an analyst who has studied Russian trolling efforts, "I don't think social media companies have come up with an automated way to filter out this content yet."[12]

As more people get their news from social media, the problem of fake news continues to grow. The phenomenon ranges from relatively harmless stories like false claims for health foods to serious attempts to undermine political beliefs and elections. Fake news stories that appear on social media news feeds then go viral by way of sharing and reposting. Fake news sources use outrageous headlines as clickbait to attract readers. Growing numbers of fake news websites are designed to look like legitimate news sources. Technical deceptions are used to lure readers to fake news sites. Bots, or robotic social media accounts, spread fake news through programmed activity, while trolls infiltrate social media groups with false stories and inflammatory rhetoric. Experts say all these methods of spreading fake news makes the job of finding the truth even more challenging for the public. "It can be exhausting for people to have to try and sift through what's accurate, and what's not," says Michelle Amazeen, assistant professor of mass communication at Boston University. "But in today's age, it is in our interest to be able to determine where information is coming from so we'll recognize all the attempts at influencing us."[13]

"In today's age, it is in our interest to be able to determine where information is coming from so we'll recognize all the attempts at influencing us."[13]

—Michelle Amazeen, assistant professor of mass communication at Boston University

CHAPTER TWO

The Threat of Fake News in Politics

There is an old saying that a lie can travel halfway around the world before the truth gets its boots on. In other words, fake news spreads much faster than the truth. According to a study published in the March 9, 2019, issue of *Science*, that old saying is basically correct, especially for political news. The research was conducted by Soroush Vosoughi and two colleagues for the Media Lab at the Massachusetts Institute of Technology. The study's authors looked at 126,000 true and false stories spread on Twitter from 2006 to 2017. The stories were retweeted 4.5 million times by more than 3 million users. The study discovered that false stories spread much more rapidly than genuine ones. It also found that the top fake news stories reached as many as one hundred thousand people, compared to only about one thousand people for real news. Overall, false stories were 70 percent more likely to be retweeted than true ones. As the authors note, "Falsehood diffused significantly farther, faster, deeper, and more broadly than the truth in all categories of information, and the effects were more pronounced for false political news than for false news about terrorism, natural disasters, science, urban legends, or financial information."[14]

"Falsehood diffused significantly farther, faster, deeper, and more broadly than the truth in all categories of information, and the effects were more pronounced for false political news."[14]

—Media Lab at the Massachusetts Institute of Technology 2019 report on Twitter

Evidently, many people are ready to believe and spread false political stories, preferring the novelty of the lie to the less exciting truth. The study shows the growing threat that fake news in politics represents for democracy in America.

Fake News and the Ballot Box

Voters need accurate information to make informed decisions. When voters are misled by fake news stories, the results show up in national polls and at the ballot box. A voter may support or reject a candidate on the basis of fake news picked up online or shared on social media. Bombarded with half-truths, deceptive claims, and outright lies, people can become confused about which stories are legitimate. Many voters despair over ever finding the truth. Polls show that fake news, in all its manifestations on the internet and social media, has become a major concern for Americans. A Pew Research Center survey released in June 2019 revealed that adults in the United States consider fake news a more serious problem than violent crime, climate change, or terrorism. More than half of those surveyed said they have encountered fake news online. Many reported changing their internet search habits to avoid what they considered false political stories.

The growth of fake news also helps make voters more cynical. It can lead people to regard all national media with suspicion. A September 2019 Gallup poll showed that only 41 percent of Americans trust the mass media. Moreover, an even greater divide exists between the two major political parties. Only 15 percent of Republicans expressed trust in the media, compared to 69 percent of Democrats. And distrust of the media can translate into a larger distrust of America's democratic system of government. The Pew Research Center survey reported that 70 percent of Americans feel that fake news and misinformation have eroded their confidence in the government.

Another way that fake news can influence voters is the so-called echo chamber effect. Faced with a bewildering array of political stories, many people turn to news sources that suit their own political biases. Their news diet becomes like an echo chamber that repeats the same thing over and over. These individuals are much more likely to post or retweet stories that align with their beliefs—even if the stories are false, biased, or unproven. A similar concept is the filter bubble. Social media users interact within bubbles that include only people who share their interests and agree with them politically. Such people automatically share or retweet stories that confirm their beliefs. "Humans tend to prefer ideas that we agree with. We just do," says David Weinberger, senior researcher at Harvard's Berkman Klein Center for Internet & Society. "In a network as large as the Internet, we could spend the rest of our lives trapped in endless loops of sameness, convincing ourselves that we're right and everyone else is an idiot."[15] As a result, fewer voters today are weighing competing policies and ideas before casting their ballots. And some hard-core partisans, extremist groups, and foreign trolls fuel this tendency by spreading fake news.

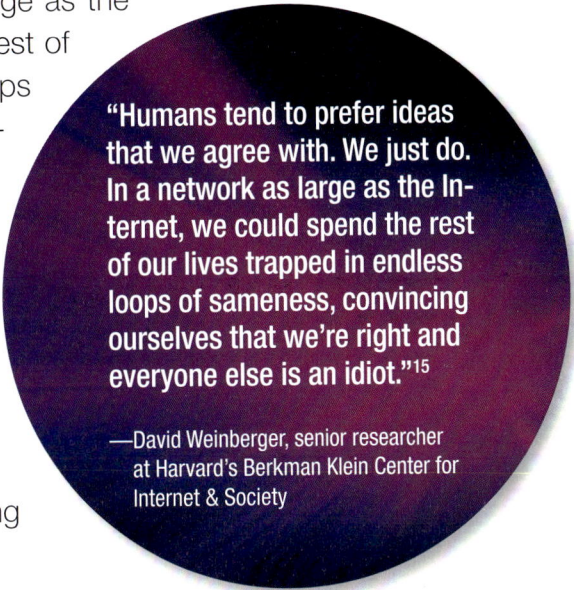

> "Humans tend to prefer ideas that we agree with. We just do. In a network as large as the Internet, we could spend the rest of our lives trapped in endless loops of sameness, convincing ourselves that we're right and everyone else is an idiot."[15]
>
> —David Weinberger, senior researcher at Harvard's Berkman Klein Center for Internet & Society

Trump's Attacks on the Media

Controversy over fake news in politics has exploded in recent years due in large part to Trump's attacks on the media. In fact, in 2017 Trump told an interviewer he actually invented the term *fake news*. He did not—the term has been around for years—but he has successfully weaponized it through his tweets and rally speeches. In a November 8, 2018, confrontation at a White House press conference, Trump told a reporter from CNN, "When you report fake news, which CNN does a lot, you are the enemy of the people."[16] Afterward, the White

At a news conference in November 2018, President Donald J. Trump (right) accuses CNN reporter Jim Acosta (left) of working for a network that reports "fake news." Trump often deems any news that does not portray him or his administration in a positive light as fake.

House banned CNN's Jim Acosta from future press conferences. Trump frequently refers to reporters who criticize him as fake news, and he contends that the press does not cover his administration fairly.

At the same time, Trump has repeatedly been caught making false statements himself. As of October 14, 2019, fact-checkers at the *Washington Post* claimed he had made more than 13,400 false or misleading statements since taking office. He has tweeted bogus statistics about crime among minorities and immigrants, falsely claimed to have created the strongest economy ever, and made exaggerated attacks on longtime US allies and dozens of political enemies. Trump's verbal assaults on the press, combined with his own habit of spreading falsehoods, only serve to increase the public's distrust and cynicism regarding media and the government. Some critics believe this is part of his plan. "What

Trump wants is for you to no longer have any critical faculties and discernment," says Ruth Ben-Ghiat, a history professor at New York University. "You don't know what to believe, so you believe him. This has worked, unfortunately, over and over again over the years. It's a very dangerous cycle that we're in now. It's been an enormous learning curve for the journalism profession, for citizens, and for every sector of society."[17]

As for Trump's supporters, they remain as loyal as ever. To them fake news is mostly the work of a hostile press that is biased against an administration it despises. They point to a 2018 Media Research Center report that found network news coverage of Trump to be 92 percent negative. Meanwhile, the strong economy and historically low unemployment numbers received less than 1 percent of total coverage. As Jean Feaser, a retired factory worker, said at an October 2018 Trump rally in Fort Myers, Florida, "I never considered the news being fake until Trump became president."[18]

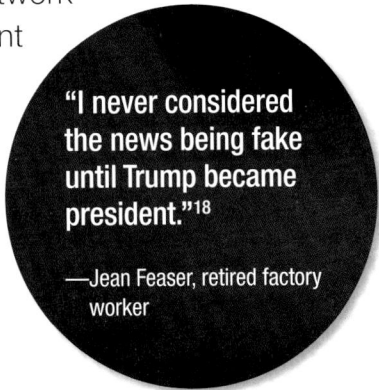

> "I never considered the news being fake until Trump became president."[18]
>
> —Jean Feaser, retired factory worker

Russian Trolls and Bots

Efforts to mislead American voters with fake news are led in part by foreign trolls. In the 2016 US election campaign, Russian military officers operating with the IRA spread propaganda and disinformation on social media platforms such as Facebook, Twitter, and Instagram. Russian trolls planted fake news stories about racist incidents and social unrest in the United States in an attempt to demoralize minority voters. They mounted attacks on Democratic presidential nominee Hillary Clinton and promoted the Trump agenda. They declared that the American electoral system was rigged and urged voters to boycott the election. Russian bots, or programmed social media accounts, bounced outrageous fake news stories back and forth to every corner of the social media platforms.

Former special counsel Robert Mueller testifies to Congress in July 2019. Mueller's report described Russian efforts to mislead American voters with disinformation and propaganda. Such operations are intended to sow discord among Americans and undermine trust in American institutions.

In his report on Russian electoral interference, Robert Mueller described the IRA's disinformation campaign in detail. The Russian trolls had created fake social media accounts designed to look like they were managed by American political groups and activist organizations. When others, including campaign officials and media figures, retweeted the Russian stories, they spread like wildfire. The IRA even managed to attract Trump supporters to fake campaign events they set up in Florida and Pennsylvania. Many mainstream American news outlets were deceived and used tweets from the IRA in their own stories on the election.

Pushing fake news is a specialty of the Russian intelligence agencies going back to the Soviet era. The goal is to sow discord among Americans and undermine trust in American institutions. Russian trolling efforts were muted in the 2018 midterm elections.

Nonetheless, media experts predicted that Russia and other foreign governments would use an onslaught of trolls once more to influence the 2020 presidential election. In October 2019 Facebook officials reported that personas created in Russia had begun organizing a network of fake accounts in January on Instagram, which is owned by Facebook. The accounts were designed to look like the work of American political groups in swing states, or states that were likely to be closely contested in 2020. The Russian accounts appeared to have sprung from all points of the political spectrum, but most of them criticized the candidacy of former vice president Joe Biden. Many of the accounts had user names that mimicked black activist organizations or LGBTQ rights groups. According to Facebook, the network of Russian-based accounts already had 250,000 followers. How many of these were Russian bots is unclear.

Facebook announced that it had shut down the network of Russian accounts in its early stages and shared information about the accounts with law enforcement. Graphika, a social media investigations company hired by Facebook, noted that social media companies are making it more difficult for Russian trolls to set up shop for election interference. "People in Russia are still trying this," says Ben Nimmo, one of Graphika's lead investigators. "In 2016, you could have set up an account posing as a Tennessee Republican and have it registered to a Russian phone number."[19] Now, Nimmo believes, such a ploy is more likely to be spotted and foiled.

Fake News from Extremist Groups

Homegrown trolls also are responsible for spreading fake news related to politics. Many of these are extremist groups seeking to discredit their political foes and lure like-minded readers to believe false narratives. Some of the groups are dedicated to spreading messages of hate and violence. For example, the far-right message board 4chan is notorious for distributing racist, anti-Semitic, and terrorism-related posts that attract like-minded extremists from social media and across the internet. Trolls from 4chan often

Creating Fake Political News for Profit

With such a ready audience for political news in America, some foreign trolls are churning out fake news stories to make money. One troll farm for profit is located in Veles, Macedonia, a nation in eastern Europe. In 2016 more than one hundred fake news websites were traced to this quiet riverside village, most of them pushing stories favorable to Donald Trump's campaign. The success of these operators is judged by the number of clicks their bogus stories generate. Each click they get from American political junkies helps boost their bank accounts. Many of the stories are outrageously false, claiming a candidate has admitted to murder or been hospitalized after a car crash—whatever it takes to attract interest on social media.

Macedonian trolls claim they can make $2,500 a day from ads on their websites. The revenue comes from AdSense, a Google service that distributes targeted ads around the internet. According to a CNN report, the Macedonians are already gearing up for the 2020 election, hiring workers to produce reams of fake news material to share. Mirko Ceselkoski teaches young people in Veles how to make a good living targeting Americans in the fake news industry. Some of his charges have become millionaires through fake news. The trick, says Ceselkoski, is creating a Facebook profile and then joining an influential group with a political focus. "They tag their friends and argue with them," he says, "and the story spreads even more."

Quoted in Derrick A. Paulo and Daniel Heng, "Meet the Fake News Trolls Who Influenced US and Indonesian Polls for Money," CNA, January 5, 2019. www.channelnewsasia.com.

spread disinformation about stories in the news. For example, they posted lies about a mass shooting that took place on October 1, 2017, leaving fifty-eight people dead and more than five hundred wounded at a country music concert in Las Vegas, Nevada. Four different 4chan trolls made a false identification of the shooter and claimed he was a partisan Democrat. Somehow the 4chan story appeared in Google's search results before its source was discovered and removed.

In August 2019 twenty-eight-year-old Josh Goldberg fell victim to a 4chan scam. Goldberg received anxious calls from friends warning him that someone was using his image on a fake Twitter account. Trolls from 4chan had copied Goldberg's photo from his Facebook page, where he promotes his performances of traditional Jewish music. The trolls then used the photo in creating a Twitter account for "Adam Greenblatt," in which they tweeted anti-Semitic messages and urged divestment from Israel. Goldberg soon discovered that the 4chan trolls were responsible for a string of fake Twitter accounts purporting to be Orthodox Jews. "They wanted to masquerade as Jewish people and sow the seeds of division,"[20] says Goldberg.

Policing extremist trolls on social media and internet message boards is a huge challenge. When 4chan trolls felt the heat from adverse publicity, they migrated to other boards, such as the radical site Telegram, a meeting place for right-wing street gangs, and one dubbed 8chan. Cloudflare, a content delivery and security network, cut off service for 8chan following reports of its violent content. But Cloudflare chief executive officer (CEO) Matthew Prince has warned that it is almost impossible to eliminate extremist sites that specialize in fake news. When kicked off one hosting site, they simply relocate to some other unused corner of the internet. As Prince explains, "Almost exactly two years ago we made the determination to kick another disgusting site off CloudFlare's network: The Daily Stormer. . . . Today, the [neo-Nazi] Daily Stormer is still available and still disgusting. They have bragged that they have more readers than ever."[21]

> "Almost exactly two years ago we made the determination to kick another disgusting site off CloudFlare's network: The Daily Stormer. . . . Today, the [neo-Nazi] Daily Stormer is still available and still disgusting. They have bragged that they have more readers than ever."[21]
>
> —Matthew Prince, Cloudflare CEO

Trolling with Artificial Intelligence

Political trolls, both foreign and domestic, now have technological tools that make use of artificial intelligence (AI). Russian bots employ AI to mimic the social media behavior of other accounts.

Like Facebook itself, they use AI and sophisticated algorithms to tailor news and advertisements to a user's political profile. Now trolls are creating so-called deepfakes, which are videos that are altered to present fake content. Deepfake technology uses machine learning to doctor video images with different faces and voices. Unlike the Photoshopped memes from recent elections, the changes are so subtle that they can fool even the eyes and ears of experts.

On obscure websites, tech-savvy individuals have posted deepfakes of celebrities or former girlfriends in racy or violent videos. The website BuzzFeed demonstrated the political possibilities for deepfakes when it created a comedy video of former president Barack Obama mocking Donald Trump. The fake clip

Deepfake technology uses machine learning to doctor video images with changes so subtle that they can fool experts. US House of Representatives Speaker Nancy Pelosi (pictured) was the subject of one such deepfake video that appeared to show her slurring her speech as if intoxicated.

Detecting Fake News Videos

As deepfake videos become more sophisticated in their ability to fool viewers, the need for tech experts to expose them also grows. Computer-generated videos can rocket across social media before they can be debunked. People may assume that deepfakes are real and casually share them on social media. Research shows they tend to retain memories of fake news even after such ploys have been uncovered. Like the false controversy over Barack Obama's birth certificate, once misinformation spreads into the public forum, it is nearly impossible to eliminate. And deepfakes present a dangerous opportunity for political trolls. "We should absolutely worry about it," says Hany Farid, a computer science professor at Dartmouth College. "This will take fake news to a whole new level."

In response, digital specialists like Farid are developing new tools to detect deepfakes. For example, fake videos can be debunked by analyzing biometric data in a subject's face, such as heart rate or blink rate. If the person displays rates that vary widely or are abnormal, the video is almost certainly a deepfake.

The same tools can also be used to authenticate videos. Trump has floated the idea that a video from NBC Studios showing him using sexist language was actually a fake. Experts like Farid may be called on to counter such contentions before they can gain traction.

Quoted in Hilke Schellmann, "The Dangerous New Technology That Will Make Us Question Our Basic Idea of Reality," *Quartz*, December 5, 2017. https://qz.com.

---

superimposed Obama's face onto a video of Hollywood director Jordan Peele. A doctored video that went viral on social media featured House Speaker Nancy Pelosi slurring her speech as if she were intoxicated. Late night talk show hosts have done the same with footage of Trump speeches. Casual viewers might easily mistake deepfakes posted on social media for the real thing. Media experts worry that deepfakes could be used to announce fake policy shifts for political candidates or even to create a bogus declaration of nuclear war. According to Bobby Chesney, a University of Texas law professor who has studied the deepfake phenomenon, "The opportunity for malicious liars is going to grow by leaps and bounds."[22] Major social media sites are concerned that Russian groups like the IRA could add deepfake videos to their trolling repertoire. Facebook, YouTube, and Reddit are already working with researchers to detect and remove deep-fakes from their platforms.

Fake news presents a special problem in politics. It can mislead voters, spread confusion during the campaign season, and affect outcomes at the ballot box. Trump decries media coverage of him as fake news, even as he sometimes deals in falsehoods and half-truths himself. Social media trolls from Russia and other countries sow discord and cynicism with fake news stories and advertisements. New technologies such as AI make fake news even easier to distribute and more difficult to detect. Fake news spread by extremist groups can promote racism and violence. In trying to eliminate fake news from their platforms, social media companies face a huge challenge.

CHAPTER THREE

Fake News in Health and Science

In 2017 thirty-three-year-old Kim Nelson read a news article on her phone that set off alarm bells in her head. The article noted that in Greenville, South Carolina, exemptions for child-hood vaccinations due to religious beliefs had jumped by 70 percent. She also found stories about troubling dips in vaccination rates around the country. Having just moved to Greenville with her husband and two young daughters, Nelson felt duty bound to set the record straight about vaccinations. She knew they saved lives, and she wanted to make sure that other parents knew that fact as well. Nelson started the group South Carolina Parents for Vaccines. She posted the latest scientific articles about vaccines on social media. She organized classes at the local library. If a worried parent had questions, she was ready with personal messages and advice on where to get information. Nelson was determined to keep others from falling for fake news stories about the issue. "As somebody who just cannot stand wrong things being on the internet," says Nelson, "if I saw something with vaccines, I was very quick to chime in 'That's not true' or 'No, that's not how that works.' I usually got banned."[23]

"As somebody who just cannot stand wrong things being on the internet, if I saw something with vaccines, I was very quick to chime in 'That's not true' or 'No, that's not how that works.' I usually got banned."[23]

—Kim Nelson, concerned parent in Greenville, South Carolina

Debunked Stories About Vaccine Risks

The anti-vaccination movement—or anti-vaxx, for short—shows how fake news related to health care can have dangerous effects. The controversy dates to 1998, when a British doctor named Andrew Wakefield and two colleagues published a paper claiming that the vaccine for mumps, measles, and rubella (called MMR) caused some children to develop autism. After a review, medical experts found that the paper was based on fraudulent studies and misleading data. A second paper by Wakefield and his co-workers claiming links between the vaccine for measles virus and autism was also found to be bogus. Both papers were struck from the scientific record. Wakefield was stripped of his medical license in the United Kingdom. Subsequent studies affirmed that MMR vaccines are indeed safe and do not cause autism.

Nonetheless, the panic over vaccinations not only persisted but grew. The fact that some children who developed autism had also received the MMR vaccine led certain parents to mistakenly assume a link between the two. In 2016 Wakefield released a pseudoscientific documentary film titled *Vaxxed*. The film claimed

The spread of fake news about the dangers of the childhood measles, mumps, and rubella vaccine has led to thousands of parents in the United States refusing to vaccinate their children against these illnesses. Experts fear this could result in a deadly outbreak of disease.

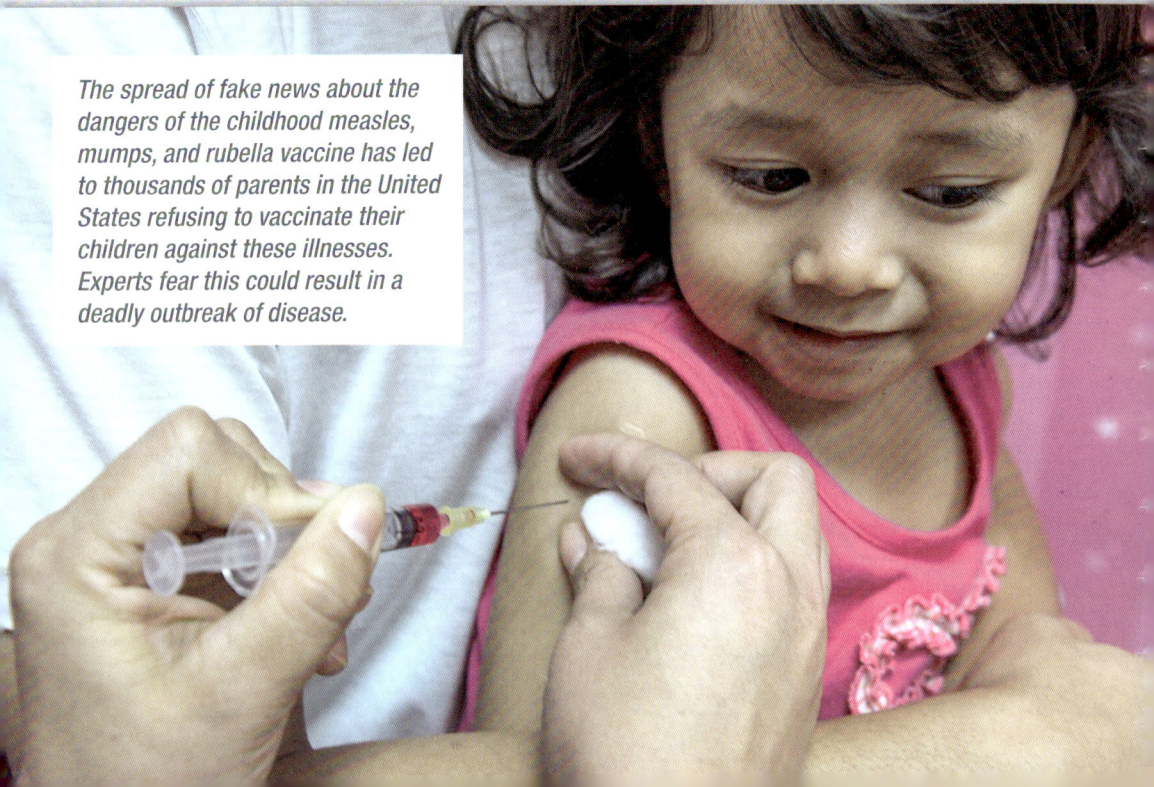

that the Centers for Disease Control and Prevention (CDC) had tried to cover up the links between MMR vaccine and autism. Celebrities and public figures—including Jenny McCarthy, Jim Carrey, Alicia Silverstone, Robert Kennedy Jr., and Jessica Biel—have voiced criticism of vaccination. Some activists have denied they are anti-vaccine but instead are only seeking safer vaccines overall. However, the anti-vaxx movement has led thousands of parents nationwide to refuse vaccinations for their children. Experts say even a few cases of disease due to children going unvaccinated can cause the outbreak of a potentially deadly virus in the population. The result has been a resurgence of diseases such as measles and polio that only recently seemed to be all but eradicated. Health officials fear the United States will suffer an eruption like the measles outbreak in Europe in 2018, in which forty-one thousand children became infected and thirty-seven died. According to Claire McCarthy, assistant professor of pediatrics at Harvard Medical School:

"We need to take a stand for the health of children. We need to speak up when people say untrue things about immunizations, especially when those people are public figures."[24]

—Claire McCarthy, assistant professor of pediatrics at Harvard Medical School

> We need to take a stand for the health of children. We need to speak up when people say untrue things about immunizations, especially when those people are public figures. We need to work legislatively so that the only children in school who aren't vaccinated are those who have a medical reason for not getting them. We have to stand firm against alternative facts—at the same time as we reach out a hand to those who believe them.[24]

Vaccination is one of the most successful medical efforts in history. It strengthens a child's immune system to help it fight

Fake News Websites Selling Smart Pills

Many people would jump at the chance to take a pill that instantly makes them smarter and more focused mentally. Aging baby boomers who might have trouble remembering where they left their car keys present an especially large market for so-called cognitive enhancement. A dietary supplement called Geniux claimed to have the perfect solution. For a fifty-seven-dollar bottle, purchasers could improve both short-term and long-term memory, increase mental focus by 300 percent, and even increase IQ by 100 percent. Geniux was marketed with slick online ads and fake websites formatted to look like genuine news sites. The Geniux websites cited nonexistent clinical trials that supposedly had affirmed the product's amazing benefits. The websites also featured phony testimonials from customers and wrongfully included scientists and tech giants among the product's success stories, including physicist Stephen Hawking, Microsoft founder Bill Gates, and Tesla CEO Elon Musk. The websites made false promises of risk-free trials and 100 percent money-back guarantees. Social media helped spread the Geniux propaganda for free.

In April 2019, the Federal Trade Commission (FTC) announced that Geniux was a fraud. Twelve firms and four individuals were banned from making false health-related claims in the future and fined more than $600,000. In its ruling, the FTC noted it was targeting fake news websites. According to Andrew Smith, director of the FTC's Bureau of Consumer Protection, "The FTC will hold companies accountable when they deceptively design their ads to look like news articles and fabricate celebrity endorsements and consumer testimonials."

Quoted in Federal Trade Commission, "Geniux Dietary Supplement Sellers Barred from Unsupported Cognitive Improvement Claims," April 10, 2019. www.ftc.gov.

serious infections. Prior to vaccines, diseases like mumps, measles, and polio were commonplace. They were also deadly, killing thousands of people every year. It is estimated that vaccination has reduced deaths from infectious diseases by 99 percent. Before the measles vaccine was introduced in 1963, up to 4 million children a year contracted the disease. By 2000 measles had been eliminated in the United States.

Some children do get mild side effects from vaccines, such as low-grade fever or pain at the injection site. However, it is extremely rare for a child to have side effects that are severe or long lasting. Fear, based on fake news and false information, has led a surprising number of otherwise well-informed people to question the safety of vaccines. Vaccination rates in some communities are falling below the 90–95 percent level needed to prevent outbreaks of infectious disease. The problem is especially urgent in crowded urban areas, where viruses can spread rapidly. With such outbreaks considered a thing of the past, parents may fail to recognize the real health risks of not getting their children immunized.

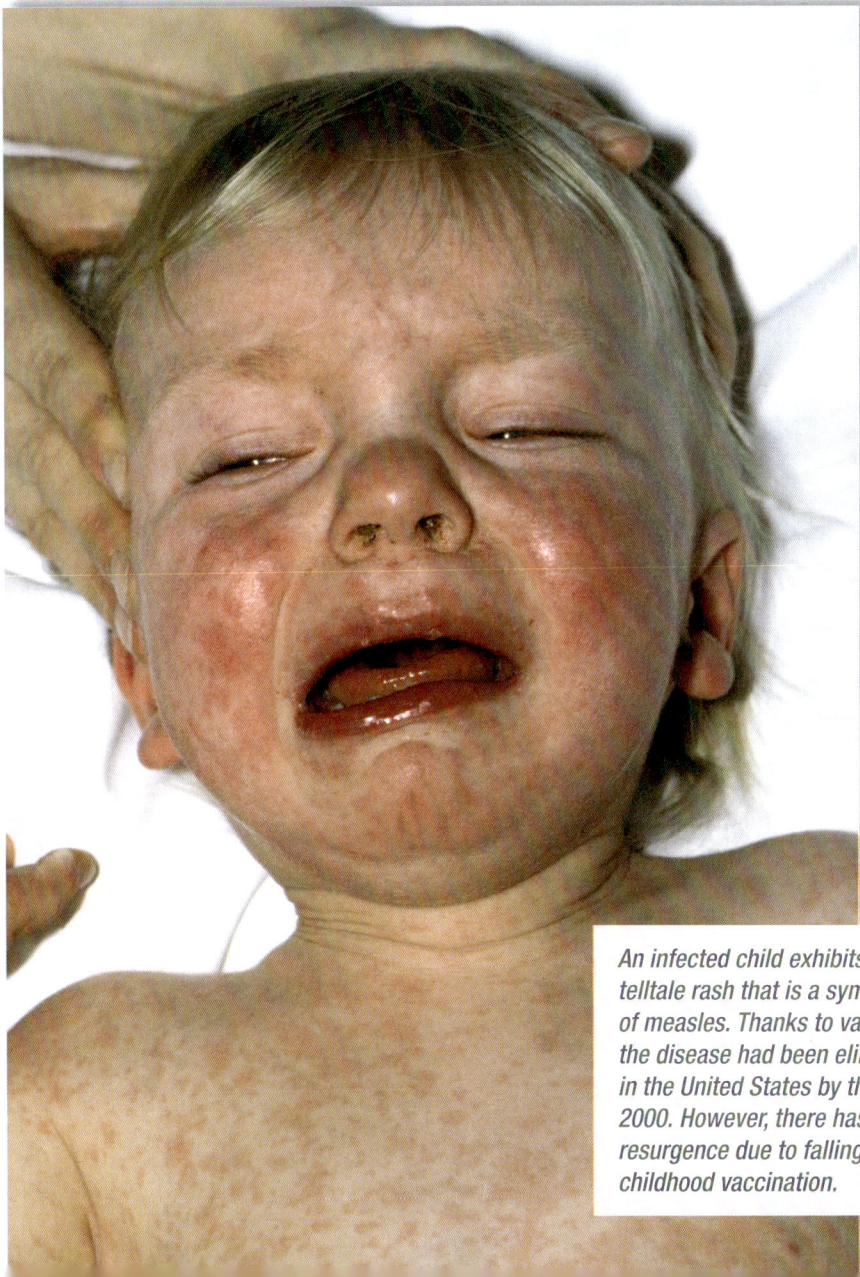

An infected child exhibits the telltale rash that is a symptom of measles. Thanks to vaccines, the disease had been eliminated in the United States by the year 2000. However, there has been a resurgence due to falling rates of childhood vaccination.

Googling Health Topics

Weighing health risks often sends people online. The internet has become an all-purpose source of information on all kinds of topics, including personal health. A 2019 study by the Pew Internet & American Life Project found that 80 percent of internet users have searched online for health-related topics. Women and the well educated are more likely to conduct such searches. Many people turn to the internet to diagnose a personal condition or evaluate a medical treatment or procedure. According to the *Philadelphia Inquirer*'s Tom Avril, this phenomenon has become known as "asking Dr. Google."[25] Physicians are often confronted by patients who believe they are well informed about a procedure or medication after an evening of web surfing. There are certainly respected medical websites that deliver solid facts, such as those of the CDC and the Mayo Clinic. However, there are also scores of sites that feature fake health news and misleading data. Health Feedback and the Credibility Coalition, which are groups of scientists that sort fact from fiction in medical media coverage, found that seven of the top ten most-shared health articles online in 2018 were either misleading or contained false information. Fake health care websites can endanger patients with serious health problems by recommending quack medicines or sowing doubts about proven medical procedures. Many sites are more focused on marketing products than providing solid information.

Doctors vary in their attitude toward patients doing their own online research. Some believe it can help a patient understand his or her condition more clearly. However, others worry that patients will fall prey to the large amount of alarmist, incomplete, or misleading information on the web. Many physicians recognize that online research about health care can have benefits—within limits. "The Internet is a tool," says Rajnish Mago, a psychiatrist at Thomas Jefferson University Hospital in Philadelphia. "You can use the tool appropriately or you can misuse it. I don't think people should diagnose themselves, but they should use the internet to become educated."[26]

False Stories About Statins and Cancer Treatments

Using the internet for self-diagnosis can lead to confusion and anxiety. Fake scare stories continue to circulate online about effective medical treatments. A good example is statin therapy. Statins are drugs that lower blood cholesterol and help prevent cardiovascular disease. They are commonly used to treat serious conditions such as diabetes. Numerous studies have affirmed their role in lowering a patient's risk for heart attack and stroke. Yet many online sources claim that side effects associated with statins are potentially life threatening and outweigh the benefits. In an editorial for *JAMA Cardiology* in June 2019, Ann Marie Navar of the Duke Clinical Research Institute compared the statin alarmists to anti-vaxxers. "While headlines shine the spotlight on vaccine refusal," wrote Navar, "the same fake medical news and fearmongering also plague the cardiovascular world through relentless attacks on statins."[27]

"The Internet is a tool. You can use the tool appropriately or you can misuse it. I don't think people should diagnose themselves, but they should use the internet to become educated."[26]

—Rajnish Mago, psychiatrist at Thomas Jefferson University Hospital in Philadelphia

Like so many medications, statins do indeed have side effects. Although for most people statins are extremely safe and effective, some patients who take them do experience muscle pain or weakness, digestive problems, mental confusion, and, in rare cases, liver damage. Yet many websites and social media posts exaggerate these risks, which are rare. They also make wild assertions that have no basis in fact, claiming that statins cause cancer, Lou Gehrig's disease, pancreatic disease, and cataracts. Some make

Detecting Fake News Videos

In the summer of 2018 a two-minute video went viral on social media, garnering more than 7 million views. To a background of peppy electronic music, a title screen in bold type announced: "This NATURAL TRICK can CURE YOUR CANCER." The video went on to describe an incredible cure for cancer that has been around since the early 1800s. In 1816, it explained, a scientist named Johan R. Tarjany discovered a rare species of moss that could "selectively alter the double helix of cancer cell DNA." According to the video, pharmaceutical companies have withheld this miraculous treatment.

The video's tantalizing pitch had one big flaw: it was entirely fake. Unlike most such videos, the makers of this video made sure viewers knew it was fake when they revealed that they had used a made-up name and that photographs of the "scientist" were actually photos of two different men. They also noted that the discovery of DNA's double helix shape did not occur until 1953, long after the year cited for Tarjany's miraculous discovery. Finally, the point of the video was revealed when it stated succinctly: "Be skeptical. Ask questions."

That message came from fake-science fighters Jonathan Jarry and his colleagues at Canada's McGill University Office for Science and Society. Jarry hopes to encourage people to be more skeptical about claims made online. "All of these clues were there to show just how easy it is to make unsubstantiated claims," says Jarry. "It's very easy to fall for these lies if you're not paying attention."

Quoted in Brian Bennett, "A 'Cancer Cure' Video Skewered Bad Science—and Went Viral Itself," *Wired*, July 10, 2018. www.wired.com.

the false argument that lowering cholesterol is actually harmful. Medical experts also note that when patients read misinformation about side effects, as with fake news about statins, they are much more likely to experience those symptoms themselves. According to Corey Bradley, another researcher at the Duke Clinical Research Institute, "There is so much misinformation about statins in the media that it's clearly permeated and now is affecting people's ability to take these medications and improve their cardiovascular health."[28]

Social media is also awash in fake news about cancer treatments. Advertisements for exotic and expensive cancer treatments claim miraculous results. At the same time, false stories about traditional therapies erode patients' trust in proven treatments. When cancer victims seek out therapies from fake scientists, the results can be disastrous. In July 2019 the head of an alternative cancer clinic in Bracht, Germany, was found guilty of causing the deaths of two people from the Netherlands and one from Belgium. The pseudo doctor, Klaus Ross, injected the patients with an overdose of 3-BP, a special molecule that has shown evidence of fighting cancer but has yet to undergo clinical trials. One of the patients had learned about Ross's clinic on the internet after reading about a fake study that convinced her to reject chemotherapy.

According to research in the October 2018 issue of *JAMA Oncology*, cancer patients who abandon their regular therapy for alternative cures, such as aromatherapy or dietary supplements, are more than twice as likely to die in the same period as patients who stick with conventional treatments. Nonetheless, social media sites like Facebook and YouTube are flooded with stories and ads about bogus cancer therapies. Both sites have announced efforts to remove false health-related content. As Fumiko Chino, an oncologist at Duke Cancer Institute, observes, "The granule of truth behind some of these can be very persuasive and can be manipulated by people who are trying to sell."[29]

Disinformation on Science News

Like medical news, science reporting presents another area where false stories and disinformation can confuse readers. In February 2018 researchers at Iowa State University (ISU) revealed that Russian trolls had been pushing fake science articles on social media. The stories question the safety of crops planted with genetically modified organisms (GMOs). Russia is one of thirty-six nations that has outlawed GMOs. Apparently, the Russian campaign to discredit the science behind GMOs had two main objectives. First, it presented Russian non-GMO produce as a safer, more environmentally friendly option for world markets. Second, it sought to increase the bitter divide over GMO science inside the United States. One Russian-based story claimed that genetically modified mosquitoes were responsible for outbreaks of the deadly Zika virus. Frank Giles, editor of *Florida Grower* magazine and an expert on the produce industry, says the ISU research demonstrates the success of the Russian fake news campaign. "My social media feeds certainly show that division between the pro- and anti-GMO forces," says Giles. "And, it is frustrating when you see much of it is based on emotion and often false information."[30]

Most experts regard GMOs as a tremendous breakthrough in genetic research. Scientists have made genetic changes to food crops to increase their resistance to insects, diseases, and drought. Over the past twenty years, use of GMOs has resulted in healthier

Researchers revealed in 2018 that Russian disinformation efforts were spreading the fake news that genetically modified mosquitoes were responsible for spreading the deadly Zika virus. These efforts were part of a larger campaign to discredit the science behind genetically modified organisms (GMOs).

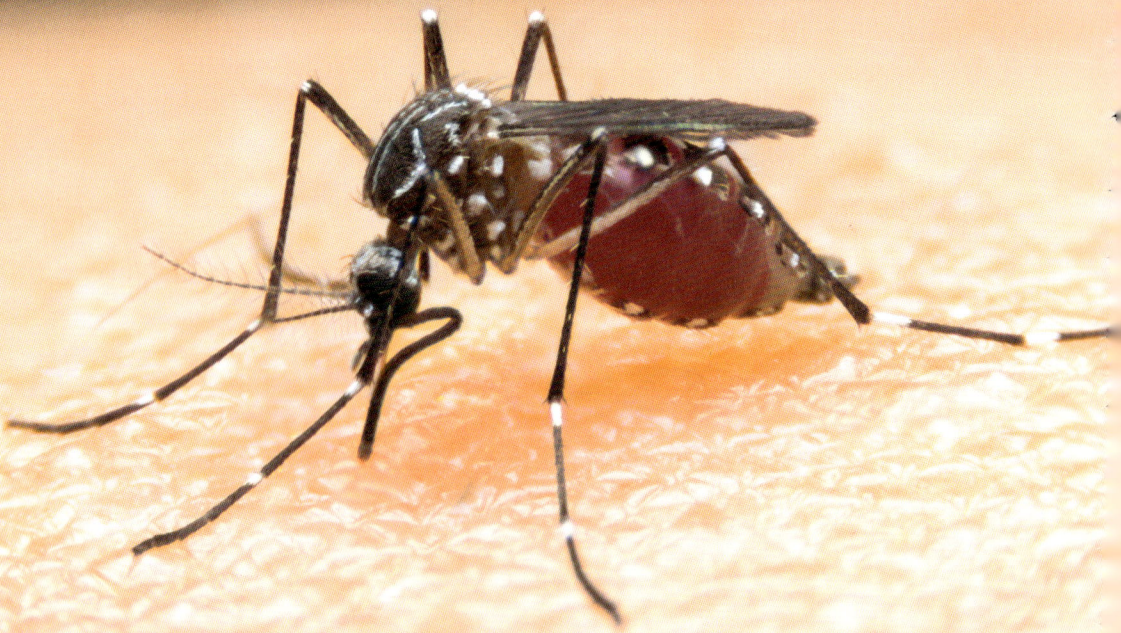

crops and larger yields for many farmers. In 2016 the National Academy of Sciences published a review of nearly one thousand studies on GMOs, concluding that they are just as safe as conventional crops. A massive 2017 study by PG Economics, an agricultural research service, found that GMO crops not only expanded food production but also helped reduce greenhouse gas emissions on corporate farms. Many GMO crops also require less land and less irrigation than unmodified crops.

Despite these findings and assurances of safety, anti-GMO forces remain bitterly opposed to what they refer to as Frankenfoods. They claim that large biochemical firms are lying about the safety of GMOs. These individuals believe genetically modified foods are a dangerous health risk for humans as well as a threat to the environment. Moreover, many Americans have come to agree with the GMO critics. A 2018 Pew Research Center report found that 49 percent of Americans believe GMOs are worse for one's health than non-GMOs. And Russia feeds into this panic about GMOs with its own propaganda, like the 2018 documentary *The Peril on Your Plate*. Experts worry that the truth about GMOs is being drowned out by all the disinformation. "Anti-GMO messaging is a wedge issue not only within the U.S. but also between the U.S. and its European allies, many of whom are deeply skeptical of GMOs," says Shawn Dorius, an assistant sociology professor who led the ISU study. "Stirring the anti-GMO pot would serve a great many of Russia's political, economic and military objectives."[31]

Overcoming Ignorance and Bias

Fake news about a complex topic like GMOs can be difficult to spot for readers with no special knowledge in biology or genetics. The same goes for many subjects related to health care or science. Nonscientists can easily be swayed by misleading arguments. Such individuals lack the necessary background to spot false or exaggerated claims. People must depend on qualified experts to debunk fake news about climate change, energy production, genetic engineering, and hundreds of other specialized subjects. Voters need to be informed in order to make reasonable decisions on these issues at the ballot box.

At the same time, scientists themselves have to avoid pitfalls related to groupthink and bias. More than a century ago, an obscure German meteorologist named Alfred Wegener suggested that the continents had once formed a huge supercontinent that had gradually drifted apart. Geologists of the time scorned reports about Wegener's theory as the epitome of fake news—an amateur's ramblings on a topic about which he knew little. Yet Wegener's theory of continental drift eventually was proved correct, along with the related discovery of tectonic plates. Pitched battles—of the intellectual type—in medicine and science are often required to get at the truth.

Fake news in medicine and science can be a threat to public health. Anti-vaccination propaganda has led many parents to decide against getting their children immunized, resulting in the resurgence of diseases that had been nearly eradicated. Patients are often fooled by false scare stories online about medications and procedures that are proved to be safe and effective. Fake news stories about scientific topics, such as genetically modified foods, also sow confusion and incite panic among consumers. People can easily be misled into believing fake reports on the internet and social media. "Science isn't about 'belief,'" says Judith Curry, former chair of the School of Earth and Atmospheric Sciences at the Georgia Institute of Technology. "It's about facts, evidence, theories, experiments. . . . 'Belief' doesn't really enter into it."[32]

> "Science isn't about 'belief.' It's about facts, evidence, theories, experiments. . . . 'Belief' doesn't really enter into it."[32]
>
> —Judith Curry, former chair of the School of Earth and Atmospheric Sciences at the Georgia Institute of Technology

CHAPTER FOUR

How Fake News Affects Teens

For a May 2018 science fair in Pennsylvania, sixteen-year-old Ryan Beam presented a scientific way to combat fake news. The Santa Cruz, California, teen designed an experiment using ten articles gathered from around the internet. Seven of the articles were genuine news, while three had been debunked by fact-checker websites. Beam placed the articles into three separate newsfeeds, or lists, like the ones on Facebook and Twitter. The first newsfeed merely offered the option to like or share each story. Its users shared the most sensational fake story more often than any of the others. The second newsfeed added a small red warning sign beside the fake stories, which made users less likely to share them. The third newsfeed obscured the headlines of the fake articles, displayed warnings that the fake stories might not be true, and required users to click a button to read them. These conditions led to the fewest shares for the articles containing fake news. Perhaps, Beam decided, there were practical ways to protect social media users—including teens—from the scourge of fake news.

Susceptible to Fake News

Since teenagers and young adults spend so much time on social media, they are especially susceptible to fake news. Distinguishing between genuine stories and fake news can be a bewildering task for teenagers. Their phones are flooded at all hours with competing facts and images. Friends on social media often share the most outrageous news stories willy-nilly with little regard for the truth. Fake or exaggerated stories often spread more rapidly than genuine news. And although teens consider themselves too savvy to be fooled by fake news, research shows the opposite. A 2016 report from the Stanford Graduate School of Education found that teens often fail to distinguish advertisements from news stories. They also struggle to identify the source of information.

Part of the problem is how teens consume news today. An August 2019 report from Common Sense Media, a nonprofit group focused on media literacy for kids, found that 54 percent of teens get their news from social media. By contrast, only 41 percent receive news from respected news organizations either in print or online. Only 37 percent consume television news even a few times a week. As far as trusting news sources, both tweens (children ages nine to twelve) and teens look to parents and other adults more than news organizations. Sixty-six percent of tweens and teens trust news they get from family, and 48 percent trust news from teachers and other adults. Only 25 percent say they trust traditional news organizations. News from friends seemed trustworthy for only 17 percent.

Teens like Beam would like to instill more trust in genuine news among young people. He notes that he is no stranger to fake news himself. "I remember one [headline] about the Pope endorsing Donald Trump," says Beam. "It was the most shared article on Facebook." The story was later shown to be fake, but he admits it nearly fooled him. "I didn't *not* believe it at first," he admits. "It seemed like it was unusual but maybe possible." Now he turns to fact-checking sites when a story seems dubious. "In school we get classes now about how to identify legitimate sources online. We're being prepared to enter the world where not everything is the truth." But like many of his peers, Beam keeps a skeptical outlook. "I take everything I read with a grain of salt."[33]

> "In school we get classes now about how to identify legitimate sources online. We're being prepared to enter the world where not everything is the truth. I take everything I read with a grain of salt."[33]
>
> —Ryan Beam, sixteen-year-old from Santa Cruz, California

Studies have shown that teens and young adults are more susceptible to fake news than older people. Teens have trouble distinguishing between real news and advertisements, and are not savvy about evaluating the credibility of information sources.

Cynicism in the Age of Trump

In the age of Trump, teens have become more cynical about the media. While the president has repeatedly attacked the mainstream press as "fake news," large numbers of teens seem to share his negative view. In December 2018 the Knight Foundation, a nonprofit group that promotes journalism and the arts, released a survey of 9,774 high school students. The survey found that 49 percent of high school students have little or no trust in the media to report news fairly and accurately. Angie, a sixteen-year-old New Yorker, believes Trump has a point about media bias. "I think this whole phenomenon has given teens awareness that bias exists and things are not what they seem,"[34] she says. Many teachers also have little confidence in media fairness. Of 498 high school teachers surveyed by the Knight Foundation, 51 percent admitted to having low levels of trust in the media. Forty percent of students admitted they trusted content posted by other people on social media more than traditional news sources.

Social media does keep young people engaged with the news in real time. Moreover, with partisan emotions running high, students are showing more interest in politics and current events. "When I started working, students weren't really interested or even knowledgeable about basic current issues," says Kathleen Carver, an AP government teacher at Wylie East High School in Texas. "Today, though, students are talking about current events. . . . Kids talk about current events and issues like it's high-school gossip. It's become a lot more relevant to them."[35]

Teens follow Trump and other prominent politicians, journalists, and pundits on Twitter. Nonetheless, most do not take Trump's outbursts too seriously. According to the *Atlantic*'s Taylor Lorenz, many students, even those who tend to be conservative, recognize that his anti-media tweets are reckless and over the top. They are quick to share his most outrageous tweets about the "fake news" media as a joke. Those who do not follow the president themselves receive screenshots of his tweets on Snapchat or Instagram. Trump's comments often wind up as punchlines and memes across social media. Sometimes the jokes even make their way into the classroom. As Carver notes, "When I say a crazy fact or something that shocks the students, I always have a student yell out 'fake news,' which causes a lot of laughter."[36]

> "When I say a crazy fact or something that shocks the students, I always have a student yell out 'fake news,' which causes a lot of laughter."[36]
>
> —Kathleen Carver, AP government teacher at Wylie East High School in Texas

Some teenaged supporters of Trump believe his tweets about fake news have a significant impact on young people. They point out how his messages reach teens without the usual media filters. But after a while teens can grow tired of all the tweets, controversy, and partisan bickering. "I can't take [Trump] seriously if he's tweeting more than I do," says Samara, a sixteen-year-old attending school in Texas. "A lot of people have him blocked."[37]

Although President Donald J. Trump is a prolific user of Twitter, some teens who follow him on the social media site say they do not take his outbursts too seriously. Social media has enabled people of all ages to keep up with the news in real time.

Turning to Trustworthy Sites

To avoid propaganda and fake news, many teens turn to news sources that have earned their trust. Young people on social media adopt a few websites, Facebook groups, or Twitter feeds that they accept as trustworthy, while tuning out nearly everything else. In the same way, they follow certain journalists whose reporting they consider to be free of bias. On Twitter they look for news accounts that have a blue check mark, indicating they are verified as authentic. Teens' attempts to be more discriminating in how they consume the news can have both good and bad results. Focusing on a few trusted social media groups may help young people avoid fake news. However, it can also lead to the echo chamber effect, in which they get their own beliefs and opinions amplified in a closed environment with no dissenting views. Some adventurous teens seek to avoid echo chambers and opinion bubbles by interacting on social media with those who have opposing views or a different outlook on controversial topics.

Teens Struggle to Detect Fake News

Young people in the United States may consider themselves to be media savvy, but most lack the ability to spot fake news on the internet and social media. That is the conclusion of a wide-ranging study of how teens and college students analyze online sources of information. A research project at Stanford's Graduate School of Education tested more than seventy-eight hundred middle school, high school, and college students in twelve states on their ability to evaluate tweets, posts, articles, photographs, and comments. Those who organized the project expressed shock at how few students were able to judge the credibility of online material.

The Stanford researchers exposed the young subjects to various kinds of fake news. Middle schoolers were shown a home page containing a traditional ad and a sponsored-content ad that looked like a news article. The students recognized the traditional ad, but over 80 percent of them mistook the sponsored-content ad for a genuine news story. Researchers presented high school students with a photograph of odd-looking daisies. The photo included a caption claiming the flowers were mutated by nuclear radiation from the Fukushima meltdown in Japan. Over 80 percent of the students accepted the photo as genuine despite its lack of attribution or explanation. The fact-checking site Snopes noted that the photograph shows a condition unrelated to nuclear radiation. "Many assume that because young people are fluent in social media they are equally savvy about what they find there," say the Stanford researchers. "Our work shows the opposite."

Quoted in Camila Domonoske, "Students Have 'Dismaying' Inability to Tell Fake News from Real, Study Finds," NPR, November 23, 2016. www.npr.org.

It's also important for teens to read actual news stories from trusted sources instead of relying on social media chatter on current events. With so many social media choices, teens often spend less time reading the news than following others' opinions about the news. "It starts as a positive, because you can get information from so many different directions," says Tolly, a sixteen-year-old blogger. "But then you'll read a headline—and you think, what's that about? And you don't click on the link—instead, you just read what other people are saying."[38]

Flop Accounts and Alternative News Outlets

Teens are also gathering on social media sites other than Facebook or Twitter to exchange political views. In part they are rejecting their parents' sites in favor of something fresh and exciting. Instagram, once known mainly as an artsy site, hosts so-called flop accounts—pages managed by groups of young people who want to share strong opinions about current politics and the spread of fake news. The accounts feature photos, videos, and screenshots about "flops," or fails, such as a YouTube clip of a racist comment or some other behavior deemed unacceptable. Flop accounts attract large numbers of visitors, and many of these accounts now feature the same trolls, polarizing remarks, and misinformation as other social media. Nonetheless, many teens still consider them more trustworthy than traditional news sources.

"[Social media] starts as a positive, because you can get information from so many different directions. But then you'll read a headline—and you think, what's that about? And you don't click on the link—instead, you just read what other people are saying."[38]

—Tolly, sixteen-year-old blogger

Instagram also hosts teen-centered accounts that try to dig more deeply into the news stories of the day. Sixteen-year-old Anjali Kanda heads the Instagram account @brown.politics, which emphasizes news for and about people of color. Kanda attracts followers with polls about current stories and videos that discuss the background of current events. She tries to avoid the sensationalism of fake news by providing more depth and balance. "People also tend to reply back to stories with questions or actually wanting to start an open discussion," she says. "I've gotten some really thoughtful insights from people replying to stories."[39]

Some enterprising young people are creating their own outlets that cater to teens in search of trustworthy news. Fifteen-year-old Olivia Seltzer noticed that traditional media rarely spoke to her age group. "This massive interest in the news and politics came with an equally massive gap in the media," she says. "Traditional news sources are primarily written by and geared toward an older demographic, and unfortunately, they don't always connect to my generation."[40] In response, Seltzer started the Cramm, a newsletter that provides a daily package of major news stories from around the world. Delivered via email or text every weekday, the Cramm features stories from major outlets, including the *New York Times*, CBS, NBC, BBC, Politico, and Reuters. Seltzer and her editorial team strive to compile the most important stories of the day, along with interviews of figures in the news. The focus on legitimate sources helps the team avoid the pitfalls of fake news and misinformation. And delivering the Cramm by text enables the team to reach more teens. "I don't think other news sources or a lot of people are aware that young people don't really use email addresses," says Seltzer. "[The Cramm] is actually written by a young person, geared toward young people, and I think that's really important."[41]

Learning to Distinguish Between Genuine and Fake News

Regardless of which news sources teens seek out, they often struggle to identify fake news. According to a March 2017 survey by Common Sense Media, only 44 percent of young people feel confident they can tell fake news stories from genuine ones. In addition, 31 percent of kids who had shared a news story online within the previous six months said they found out later a story they had shared was wrong or inaccurate. Teens frequently struggle to distinguish fake news stories because such stories mimic the look of genuine news articles so successfully. Teens also lack experience in evaluating the sources for stories. The 2016 Stanford research project found that a large percentage of middle school and high school students failed to recognize photoshopped images or loaded words that indicated a story was false or biased.

The fact that fake news stories look the same as genuine ones contributes to the trouble some young people experience distinguishing between the two. According to one study, only 44 percent of young people felt confident they could tell a fake story from a real one.

Teens' inability to spot fake news can lead to a skeptical outlook about news in general. And the effect seems to hold for college students. An October 2018 survey conducted by Northeastern University found that nearly half of college students lacked confidence in identifying fake news on social media. Thirty-six percent admitted the threat of misinformation reduced their trust in all media. "Our report suggests that in some ways, we have created for young people an extremely difficult environment of news," says John Wihbey, a professor at Northeastern University and one of the study's coauthors. "We need to figure out ways to guide them so they can navigate it."[42]

As Wihbey and other experts note, teens need to be better

> "Our report suggests that in some ways, we have created for young people an extremely difficult environment of news. We need to figure out ways to guide them so they can navigate it."[42]
>
> —John Wihbey, professor at Northeastern University

Checking the Facts with Checkology

One way for students to learn how to evaluate news for truthfulness is to play the role of news gatherer. This exercise is part of the Checkology Virtual Classroom, a new educational tool developed by the News Literacy Project in Washington, DC. A total of 1.5 million students are using the Checkology curriculum worldwide. To determine the news value of a story, students gather facts on the topic independently. In the course of their research, they check whether the story is true and confirm that its sources are valid. The object is to teach teens to recognize an approach to news reporting that is balanced and objective versus one that is slanted or intended to deceive.

In Kyle Eichner's seventh grade social studies class at Wellesley Middle School in Massachusetts, students discuss current issues and examine how people tend to reject stories that contradict what they believe. They look at how images can be used to manipulate people's emotions or give a false impression about an individual or event. They also examine the reasons why certain stories go viral. Eichner's students promise to be much more discerning in how they evaluate news stories going forward. As Eichner admits, "They give me so much hope."

Quoted in Bernhard Warner, "Teenagers Are Our Best Hope in Fighting Fake News," *Boston Globe,* January 18, 2018. www.bostonglobe.com.

educated in how to spot fake news. Schools around the nation are adding media literacy programs to boost students' ability to analyze news stories for misinformation or bias. Google, which has come under fire for fake news on its own platform, has developed a new tool to help young people become more media savvy. MediaWise is a program that seeks to teach 1 million students how to distinguish fake news from real news online. Based on a curriculum created by the Stanford History Education Group, the program leads students to check photographs for signs of manipulation and use fact-checking to evaluate social media posts for accuracy. One middle school class of three hundred students learned how to discern that a viral photo of an actor tumbling down stairs at the Met Gala in New York was a photoshopped fake. The creators of MediaWise hope it will inspire students to double-check media sources by habit. "MediaWise helps teens figure out what's real and what's not by teaching them fact-checking skills that professional journalists use," says Katy Byron, the editor and program manager of the MediaWise project. "I like to think of it this way: if misinformation online is a disease, then Media-Wise is the Red Cross."[43]

Studies show that teens are susceptible to being fooled by fake news on social media. The growth of fake and misleading news tends to make young people less trusting of all news sources. Many teens are seeking out trustworthy news sites and social media groups and tuning out other news media. Some teens are creating their own news outlets and forums, designed to appeal to their own age group. Schools and social media companies like Google are trying to teach young people how to spot false stories and bogus images on the internet. As teens are deluged by information on social media, they must develop a sharp eye for fake news.

CHAPTER FIVE

Solutions to the Fake News Epidemic

In an appearance before Congress on October 23, 2019, Facebook founder and CEO Mark Zuckerberg faced heated questions about fake and misleading political ads on his platform. At one point Representative Alexandria Ocasio-Cortez, a Democrat from New York, asked if she could run Facebook ads making false claims that a Republican had voted for the Green New Deal, an environmental plan strongly opposed by nearly all Republicans. Zuckerberg replied that she probably could. "Do you see a potential problem here with a complete lack of fact-checking on political advertisements?" Ocasio asked. Shifting uncomfortably, Zuckerberg answered, "I think lying is bad, and I think if you were to run an ad that had a lie, that would be bad."[44] He went on to suggest that there was value in letting voters see for themselves that a candidate was lying. Zuckerberg seemed reluctant to have Facebook referee the rival claims made in political ads. Many voices in Congress and the media, however, have demanded that Facebook and other social media companies take action to weed out deceptive ads and fake news on their platforms.

An Urgent Responsibility

A majority of Americans agree about stopping fake news. An October 2018 HuffPost/YouGov survey found that 59 percent of respondents believe the social media giants have an urgent responsibility to stop the spread of fake news and conspiracy theories. About half of those surveyed believe the companies are not doing enough in that regard. Democrats were more than twice as likely as Republicans and Trump supporters to favor stricter content standards on social media. As the next presidential election approached, many people worried that fake news stories and ads like those posted by Russian trolls in 2016 could influence the outcome.

Faced with criticism about fake and misleading political ads, Twitter and Facebook have responded in very different ways. On October 30, 2019, Twitter CEO Jack Dorsey announced that his company would no longer accept any political ads. Dorsey said that in his opinion the reach of a political message should be earned by likes and retweets, not paid for with campaign funds. Many observers noted that the ad ban arose on Trump's favorite social media outlet. By contrast, Zuckerberg decided that Facebook would change its policy, which had banned misinformation in political ads. The company would now accept ads from politicians and political parties even when they contained apparent lies or deceptions. For Zuckerberg, the issue was free expression. "I don't think it's right for a private company to censor politicians or the news in a democracy," he said. "Like the other major internet platforms and most media, Facebook doesn't fact-check political ads. And if content is newsworthy, we won't take it down. . . . I believe we should err on the side of allowing greater expression."[45]

"Like the other major internet platforms and most media, Facebook doesn't fact-check political ads. . . . I believe we should err on the side of allowing greater expression."[45]

—Mark Zuckerberg, founder and CEO of Facebook

Zuckerberg's decision brought a storm of disapproval. Even employees at Facebook spoke out against the new policy. Progressives and left-wing pundits warned it would give Trump and the Republican Party a free hand to spread political lies and smears. To make a point, Massachusetts senator Elizabeth Warren (one of the Democrats seeking to be the party's presidential nominee), bought an ad on Facebook in which she falsely claimed Zuckerberg had endorsed Trump in the 2020 election. Later she addressed the Facebook CEO in a tweet: "It's up to you whether you take money to promote lies. You can be in the disinformation-for-profit business, or you can hold yourself to some standards. In fact, those standards were in your policy. Why the change?"[46]

Fighting Fake News on Social Media

Legally, Zuckerberg and Facebook are under no obligation to check the truth of material that appears on the site. This holds true for all social media companies. In the interest of free speech, the Telecommunications Act of 1996 provided internet firms and social media platforms the license to host misinformation as long as they did not endorse it. In other words, these companies cannot be sued or sanctioned for hosting fake news—whether news stories, mischievous bots, or deepfake videos.

Nonetheless, public outrage about fake news—especially after Russia's disinformation campaign in 2016—has led to change. Social media companies, including Facebook and Twitter, have stepped up efforts to combat fake news and false information on their platforms. Twitter places a blue check mark beside accounts that are verified as authentic. Typically these are accounts considered to be of public interest in areas such as government, politics, religion, journalism, media, sports, and business. Yet the sheer volume of posts and tweets makes it difficult to slow down the fake news epidemic. For example, an estimated 500 million tweets are sent each day, rendering editorial control all but impossible. Nevertheless, social media firms are trying new approaches that show promise for fighting fake news.

One method is to counter fake news with the truth. In December 2016 Facebook launched a program to partner with fact-checkers who scoured the platform for misleading or false content. Today that effort has grown to include forty-three fact-checking organizations around the world, operating in twenty-four different languages. Articles are flagged for possible inaccuracy by human users or by special algorithms that analyze language patterns. Facebook's algorithms scan billions of stories and posts every day in order to flag fake news before it can go viral. Fact-checkers then research certain disputed claims and write a concise paragraph to rebut any false content. Users who posted the original story are notified about its status as a fake. Those who try

In October 2019, Facebook CEO Mark Zuckerberg testified to Congress in a hearing about disinformation on the Facebook platform. Many legislators and others believe Facebook, as well as other social media companies, have a responsibility to act against deceptive ads and fake news on their platforms.

to repost articles that have been fact-checked receive a pop-up message containing the fact-checker's concerns. Researchers at Stanford University and New York University found that users have encountered fewer fake news stories on Facebook since 2017. Nonetheless, observers fear that fact-checkers are fighting a losing battle. "It's like bringing a spoon to clear out a pig farm," says P.W. Singer, senior fellow at New America, a nonpartisan think tank in Washington, DC. "Facebook is never going to be able to hire enough people, and the artificial intelligence is never going to be able to do all of this on its own."[47]

Some sites use crowdsourcing, or the combined knowledge of a large group, to assess false or misleading claims. Users can police the sites themselves, posting corrections to fake news as soon as it is spotted. The Democratic National Committee has created so-called Geek Squads to identify and correct misleading claims about its candidates on social media. There are also widely consulted fact-checking sites such as Snopes, PolitiFact, and FactCheck.org that track fake news websites and stories on social media. A recent study from the University of California, Riverside, shows that simply flagging false news stories on social media can help prevent their distribution. For example, a fake story claiming that French president Emmanuel Macron asked Twitter to suspend Trump's account for harassing others was flagged on Facebook with the tagline "Disputed by Snopes.com and Politifact."[48] The researchers found that the label significantly reduced sharing of the fake news story.

Detecting and Eliminating Bots

Another way to deal with fake news is to identify and eliminate bots, or automated accounts that spread misinformation and bogus news stories. Bots are programmed to add likes, post comments, and follow social media as though they were real users. They can also push fake stories to the top of people's news feeds and search results. Social media firms look for telltale signs to detect bots, such as sudden spikes in account activity or thousands

PØLITIFACT

AT THE POYNTER INSTITUTE | WINNER OF THE PULITZER PRIZE

EDITIONS ∨   TRUTH-O-METER™ ∨   PEOPLE ∨   PRO   PAN

ve On Mac

Apps You Shou Setapp now, with new

Over 140 top Mac app
Setapp.com

of likes compared to few or no comments. A surge in followers with newly created accounts also indicates a bot invasion. Some social media companies now require real-name registration, with users providing their legal name in order to start an account. If a company receives complaints about a particular user with an apparently fake name, it may require proof of identity, such as a driver's license.

Efforts to eliminate malicious bots picked up speed prior to the 2018 midterm elections. Facebook disabled 583 million fake profiles in the first quarter of 2018, some within minutes of the accounts being registered. Also in 2018, Twitter announced a plan to lock or remove nearly 10 million suspicious accounts per week. Instagram deletes accounts that employ apps to like or comment

The Government Should Regulate Fake News

If social media companies are unwilling to police fake news on their platforms, the government must step in. This is the view of Jessica Levinson, who is a professor and the director of the Public Service Institute at Loyola Law School, Los Angeles. Her work focuses on election law and governance issues.

> Politicians can and do post lies on social media such as Facebook and Twitter. And those companies do not have to delete those lies.
>
> In the abstract, it feels like such lies should be easy to disprove. People will simply point out the lie, and the truth will come out. In the abstract, people will not base their opinions and votes on false information they read on social media.
>
> But we don't live in the abstract. We live in reality. And in reality, what you read on social media can affect your views and votes. . . .
>
> Because media corporations appear to have no appetite to regulate this political speech, it may be up to the government to ensure that our marketplace of ideas is not corrupted by lies and deceit.

Jessica Levinson, "Facebook Has a Political Fake News Problem. Can We Fix It Without Eroding the First Amendment?," NBC News, October 24, 2019. www.nbcnews.com.

automatically. When political figures or celebrities on social media suddenly notice a severe drop in their number of followers, it often means an army of bots has been purged.

Artificial intelligence is another effective weapon against bots and fake news. AI programs use machine learning to identify fake accounts through repeated phrases or canned responses to posts. Often fake news can be identified by aggressive or emotional language that contrasts with the more reserved style of traditional news reporting. AI programs can even detect deliberately controversial comments aimed at disrupting a user group or twitter feed.

Experts warn that the AI-driven bot wars on social media are about to become even more sophisticated—and more danger-

The Government Should Not Regulate Fake News

Eliminating fake news is not the job of the government or courts. Instead, says Sandeep Gopalan, it can be accomplished through free speech and an open exchange of ideas. Gopalan is the pro vice chancellor for academic innovation and a professor of law at Deakin University, Melbourne, Australia. He argues,

> Overwhelming distrust of the once credible news media has blurred the lines between real news and falsehoods. . . .

> These problems cannot be tackled by anti–fake news laws. Courts cannot become fact-checkers and governments cannot be trusted to become arbiters of the truth through police powers. . . .

> Ultimately, legal tools should be limited to problems they can solve. Fake news is not one of these problems. The marketplace for ideas will ensure that true news trumps fake news.

> People who consume information without critical thought cannot be rescued by law and free speech should not be sacrificed in an attempt to combat fake news. Leave the laws alone.

Sandeep Gopalan, "Free Speech Cannot Be Sacrificed to Strike Fake News," *The Hill* (Washington, DC), April 6, 2018. www.thehill.com.

ous. A new AI system called GPT-2 is able to write artificial news stories that draw on current events and complex foreign policy questions. The system, built by a California-based tech firm called OpenAI as part of its research into future possibilities for artificial intelligence, can also generate photographic images to accompany the stories. Although the articles have little connection to reality, they are almost impossible to detect as fakes. For example, a GPT-2 bot could create fake news stories about the United States imposing an embargo on China, using names of real trade officials on both sides. Before the deceit was discovered, stocks could plummet and global tensions skyrocket. Foreign trolls doubtless are working on similar systems for future use. As

Sarah Kreps and Miles McCain write in *Foreign Affairs*, "Disinformation is a serious problem. Synthetic disinformation—written not by humans but by computers—might emerge as an even bigger one. Russia already employs online 'trolls' to sow discord; automating such operations could propel its disinformation efforts to new heights."[49]

Fake News and Censorship

Partisans on both the left and right worry about the effects of disinformation and fake news on social media. Across the political spectrum, people claim to support efforts by Facebook, Twitter, Instagram, and other companies to eliminate fake news. But many also fear that these efforts may lead to outright censorship. Particularly among conservatives, there is concern that political bias may guide what social media sites consider to be fake news or false statements.

Conservatives frequently complain that fact-checking sites are unreliable and almost always slanted toward the political left. They note that fact-checkers often turn to other media sources to gauge the truthfulness of statements. Yet journalists are known to make mistakes themselves, as shown by the lengthy list of corrections each day in the *New York Times*. Another objection is that fact-checking sites often check opinions on policy issues instead of facts. As editorial writer Mark Hemingway contends, "It's basically a way for a bunch of reporters with no particular expertise to render pseudoscientific judgments on statements from public figures that are obviously argumentative or otherwise unverifiable. Then there's the matter of them weighing in with thundering certitude—pants on fire!—on complex policy debates they frequently misunderstand."[50]

The News Media and Fake News

According to a June 2019 poll by the Pew Research Center, Americans blame politicians more than they blame journalists for creating false or misleading stories. However, more than half of Americans believe it is mostly the media's responsibility to fix the problem.

% of US adults who say _____ create a lot of made-up news and information

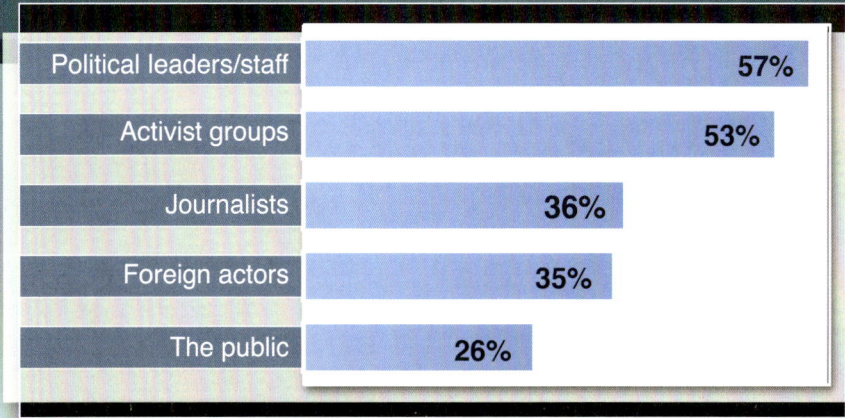

Political leaders/staff	57%
Activist groups	53%
Journalists	36%
Foreign actors	35%
The public	26%

% of US adults who say _____ have the most responsibility in reducing the amount of made-up news and information

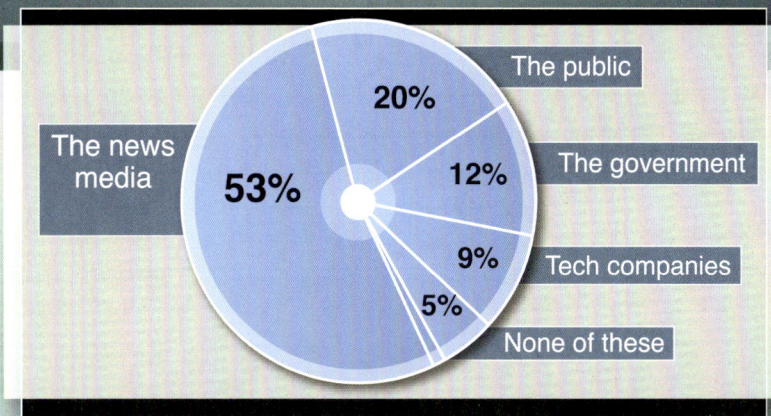

The news media 53%

The public 20%

The government 12%

Tech companies 9%

None of these 5%

Source: Pew Research Center, "Many Americans Say Made-Up News Is a Critical Problem That Needs to Be Fixed," June 5, 2019. www.journalism.org.

Political bias in fact-checking can also affect social media users' access to news. Stories may be flagged as not entirely true because of political disagreement. Yet the stories are still placed lower on Facebook's News Feed, limiting the number of viewings they receive. Facebook has acknowledged that its human reviewers make wrong calls on content in as many as one out of ten cases. Twitter and Google also admit errors, although they do not discuss actual rates.

Complaints about bias are found on both sides of the political divide. Conservatives make much of reports about left-wing bias at social media companies and tech firms. Progressives point to Zuckerberg's refusal to fact-check political ads as proof that Facebook is too friendly to Republicans. According to Jillian York, director for international freedom of expression at the Electronic Frontier Foundation, a certain amount of bias is inevitable. "Most of this content moderation is still done by humans," says York, "and humans are notorious for having their own values and biases."[51]

> "Most of this content moderation is still done by humans, and humans are notorious for having their own values and biases."[51]
>
> —Jillian York, director for international freedom of expression at the Electronic Frontier Foundation

Restoring a Sense of Trust

In a time of deep political divisions, many people are prone to believe the worst about those with whom they disagree. One side's hot exposé is dismissed by the other side as fake news. Some note that major media outlets also falsify the news by suppressing stories that are damaging to their political interests. Polls show a wide divergence when it comes to trust in the media, with liberals far more trusting than conservatives. A 2019 survey on digital news from the Reuters Institute for the Study of Journalism found that the percentage of right-wing Americans who generally trust news reporting has fallen to just

9 percent. Until this sense of trust becomes more balanced, accusations about fake news and biased journalism are likely to increase.

Since the 2016 presidential election, social media companies have focused on eliminating fake and misleading news stories and posts. They have implemented various plans, from flagging stories that are suspected of having false content to removing automated bot accounts that spread misinformation on purpose. While these efforts have generally earned approval, partisans on both the left and right worry about bias and censorship on social media platforms. With American politics so polarized, the debate about fake news and how to deal with it is certain to continue.

Introduction: Trolling the Public

1. Quoted in Craig Silverman and Scott Pham, "These Are 50 of the Biggest Fake News Hits on Facebook in 2018," BuzzFeed News, December 28, 2018. www.buzzfeednews.org.

2. Quoted in Tessa Weinberg, "Viral Post That Lottery Winner Was Arrested for Dumping Manure on Former Boss' Lawn Reeks of Falsity," PolitiFact, November 4, 2018. www.politifact.com.

3. Quoted in Michael M. Grynbaum, "Trump Calls the News Media the 'Enemy of the American People,'" *New York Times*, February 17, 2017. www.nytimes.com.

4. James Bikales, "American Media: The Nation's Watchdog," *Harvard Political Review*, December 5, 2018. www.harvard politics.com.

5. Quoted in Michelle Quinn, "US Social Media Firms Scramble to Fight Fake News," VOA, April 26, 2019. www.voanews.com.

Chapter One: How Fake News Goes Viral

6. Quoted in Kasandra Brabaw, "Celery Juice Is a Waste of Perfectly Good Produce," *Vice*, February 12, 2019. www.vice .com.

7. Quoted in Ione Wells, "Celery Juice: The Big Problem with a Viral Instagram 'Cure,'" BBC, September 22, 2019. www .bbc.com.

8. Quoted in Laura Spinney, "Fighting Ebola Is Hard. In Congo, Fake News Makes It Harder," *Science*, January 14, 2019. www.sciencemag.org.

9. Quoted in CBS News, "Don't Get Fooled by These Fake News Sites," 2019. www.cbsnews.com.

10. Quoted in Christopher Elliott, "Here Are the Real Fake News Sites," *Forbes*, February 21, 2019. www.forbes.com.

11. Quoted in Zack Budryk, "Twitter Removes 5,000 Bot Accounts Promoting 'Russiagate Hoax,'" *The Hill* (Washington, DC), April 23, 2019. www.thehill.com.

12. Quoted in Ben Popken, "Trolls for Hire: Russia's Freelance Disinformation Firms Offer Propaganda with a Professional Touch," NBC News, October 1, 2019. www.nbcnews.com.

13. Quoted in Lara Ehrlich, "The War on Fake News," COMTalk. www.bu.edu.

Chapter Two: The Threat of Fake News in Politics

14. Soroush Vosoughi et al., "The Spread of True and False News Online," *Science*, March 9, 2019. www.sciencemag.org.

15. Future of Storytelling, "The Rise of Fake News and the Crisis of Trust," April 5, 2018. www.futureofstorytelling.org.

16. Quoted in CNBC, "White House Bans CNN Reporter Jim Acosta After a Confrontation with Trump," November 8, 2018. www.cnbc.com.

17. Quoted in Gabrielle Gurley, "Can We Stop Fake News?," *American Prospect*, June 8, 2019. https://prospect.org.

18. Quoted in Daniel Bush, "When Trump Says 'Fake News,' This Is What Supporters Say They Hear," PBS, October 31, 2018. www.pbs.org.

19. Quoted in Donie O'Sullivan, "Facebook: Russian Trolls Are Back. And They're Here to Meddle with 2020," CNN Business, October 22, 2019. www.cnn.com.

20. Quoted in Jareen Imam, "4chan Trolls Impersonate Jewish People on Social Media to Spread Hate," NBC News, September 3, 2019. www.nbcnews.com.

21. Quoted in Ryan Broderick, "The Problem Isn't 8chan. It's Americans," BuzzFeed News, August 4, 2019. www .buzzfeednews.com.

22. Quoted in Sara Ashley O'Brien, "Deepfakes Are Coming. Is Big Tech Ready?," CNN, August 8, 2018. www.cnn.com.

Chapter Three: Fake News in Health and Science

23. Quoted in Alex Olgin, "How a Mother Started Her Own Vaccine Campaign to Get Rates Up," NBC News, February 25, 2019. www.nbcnews.com.

24. Claire McCarthy, "Immunization in the Era of Fake News—What Do Pediatricians Need to Do?," American Academy of Pediatrics, April 24, 2017. www.aap.org.

25. Tom Avril, "'Dr. Google' Made Me Worry About Colon Cancer. Did I Overreact?," *Philadelphia Inquirer*, September 21, 2017. www.inquirer.com.

26. Quoted in Kevin McCarthy, "The Pitfalls of Researching Symptoms Online," NueMD, April 26, 2017. www.nuemd.com.

27. Quoted in Anicka Slachta, "'The Next Target After Vaccines': Fighting Fake News About Statins," Cardiovascular Business, July 1, 2019. www.cardiovascularbusiness.com.

28. Quoted in Dennis Thompson, "Bad Info May Be Scaring Patients Away from Statins," WebMD, March 27, 2019. www.webmd.com.

29. Quoted in Daniela Hernandez and Robert McMillan, "Overrun with Bogus Cancer-Treatment Claims," *Wall Street Journal*, July 2, 2019. www.wsj.com.

30. Frank Giles, "Watch Out for Anti-GMO Fake-Out," Growing Produce, March 20, 2018. www.growingproduce.com.

31. Quoted in Wyatt Bechtel, "Russia Accused of Spreading Anti-GMO Propaganda Online," *Drovers*, February 28, 2018. www.drovers.com.

32. Judith Curry, "Why I Don't 'Believe' in 'Science,'" *Climate Etc.* (blog), March 26, 2019. https://judithcurry.com.

Chapter Four: How Fake News Affects Teens

33. Quoted in Bethany Brookshire, "Teen Fights Fake News, One Newsfeed at a Time," Science News for Students, May 18, 2018. www.sciencenewsforstudents.org.

34. Quoted in Taylor Lorenz, "Trump Has Changed How Teens View the News," *The Atlantic*, August 29, 2018. www.theatlantic.com.

35. Quoted in Lorenz, "Trump Has Changed How Teens View the News."

36. Quoted in Lorenz, "Trump Has Changed How Teens View the News."

37. Quoted in Lorenz, "Trump Has Changed How Teens View the News."

38. Quoted in Pandora Sykes, "What Is a 'Finsta'? How Fake News Is Affecting Generation Z," 2017. www.pandorasykes .com.

39. Quoted in Rainesford Stauffer, "Why Teens Are Creating Their Own News Outlets," *Teen Vogue*, August 29, 2019. www .teenvogue.com.

40. Quoted in Stauffer, "Why Teens Are Creating Their Own News Outlets."

41. Quoted in Stauffer, "Why Teens Are Creating Their Own News Outlets."

42. Quoted in Daniel Funke, "Study: Fake News Is Making College Students Question All News," Poynter Institute, October 16, 2018. www.poynter.org.

43. Katy Byron, "Helping Teens Root Out Misinformation and Get Media Savvy," Google News Initiative, January 16, 2019. www.blog.google.com.

Chapter Five: Solutions to the Fake News Epidemic

44. Quoted in Jack Kelly, "Facebook CEO Mark Zuckerberg Lambasted Before Congress over Libra, Data Privacy and Fake Political Ads," *Forbes*, October 24, 2019. www.forbes.com.

45. Mark Zuckerberg, "Facebook Stands for Free Expression," *Wall Street Journal*, October 17, 2019. www.wsj.com.

46. Quoted in Casey Newton, "Facebook's Decision to Allow Lies in Political Ads Is Coming Back to Haunt It," The Verge, October 15, 2019. www.theverge.com.

47. Quoted in Georgia Wells and Lukas I. Alpert, "In Facebook's Effort to Fight Fake News, Human Fact-Checkers Struggle to Keep Up," *Wall Street Journal*, October 18, 2018. www.wsj .com.

48. Quoted in Andrew Hutchinson, "New Study Finds That Flagging False Reports on Facebook May Indeed Reduce Their Distribution," Social Media Today, August 1, 2019. www .socialmediatoday.com.

49. Sarah Kreps and Miles McCain, "Not Your Father's Bots," *Foreign Affairs*, August 2, 2019. www.foreignaffairs.com.

50. Quoted in Investor's Business Daily, "Who Is Fact Checking the Fact Checkers?," August 2, 2018. www.investors.com.

51. Quoted in Queenie Wong, "Is Facebook Censoring Conservatives or Is Moderating Just Too Hard?," CNET, October 29, 2019. www.cnet.com.

A savvy reader should always be on the lookout for fake news or misleading information on the internet or social media. Here are a few rules to follow in order to verify that information is legitimate, unbiased, and up to date.

- Always consider the source of the story. Investigate the website, its purpose, and its sponsors.
- Look beyond the headline. A startling headline may be designed purely to get clicks.
- Check background information on the author. Consider if the person is an expert on the topic or an experienced journalist.
- Check the date of the story. Old articles may no longer be relevant or accurate.
- Consider your own biases. See if they are affecting your response to the story.
- If a story seems questionable, consult a fact-checking site or a librarian for more help.
- Examine photos and other images closely to see whether they have been manipulated.
- With outrageous stories, consider that they may be satire or intended as jokes.
- To avoid spoofing from fake news sites, bookmark favorite news sites for quick access.
- When accessing a new site, type the name into the search engine window instead of into the address field. This helps avoid being fooled by a typosquatting ruse.
- Before accessing a site, hover the mouse over a questionable domain name to see if the site looks legitimate.
- On sites related to health or science, check to see whether the information is based on scientific research or expert testimony.
- Note whether the site is focused on selling something or offering some service.

American Press Institute (API)—www.americanpressinstitute.org

The API is a national nonprofit educational organization affiliated with the News Media Alliance. One of the API's main areas of focus is so-called accountability journalism, leading a community of fact-checkers that helps build trust and knowledge among the public rather than only combating the claims of political actors.

Brookings Institution—www.brookings.edu

The Brookings Institution is a nonprofit public policy organization based in Washington, DC. Its mission is to conduct and present in-depth research on ideas for solving societal problems on the local, national, and international level. Among the many articles on its website is "How to Combat Fake News and Disinformation."

Cato Institute—www.cato.org

The Cato Institute is a public policy research organization dedicated to the principles of individual liberty, limited government, and free markets. Its scholars and analysts conduct independent, nonpartisan research on many policy issues. The Cato website features an analysis of the fake news problem titled "Fake News Is Troubling—but Censorship Is Far Worse."

Columbia Journalism Review—www.cjr.org

The *Columbia Journalism Review*'s mission is to be the intellectual leader in the rapidly changing world of journalism. It is the most respected voice on press criticism, and it shapes the ideas that make media leaders and journalists smarter about their work. It provides quick analysis and deep reporting on the tech companies and social media platforms that are shaping the media.

RAND Corporation—www.rand.org

The RAND Corporation is a research organization that develops solutions to public policy challenges. Its research and analysis address issues that impact people everywhere. Among the research articles on the RAND website is "What Role Should Schools Play in Teaching Pupils to Spot Fake News?"

Snopes—www.snopes.com

Launched in 1994, Snopes employs fact-checking and original, investigative reporting to light the way to evidence-based and contextualized analysis. Snopes always documents its sources so readers are empowered to do independent research and make up their own minds about controversial stories or claims.

Books

James W. Cortada and William Aspray, *Fake News Nation: The Long History of Lies and Misinterpretations in America*. London: Rowman & Littlefield, 2019.

Stephen Currie, *Sharing Posts: The Spread of Fake News*. San Diego, CA: ReferencePoint, 2018.

Jennifer LaGarde and Darren Hudgins, *Fact vs. Fiction: Teaching Critical Thinking Skills in the Age of Fake News*. Portland, OR: International Society for Technology in Education, 2018.

Carla Mooney, *Fake News and the Manipulation of Public Opinion*. San Diego, CA: ReferencePoint, 2019.

Cailin O'Connor and James Owen Weatherall, *The Misinformation Age: How False Beliefs Spread*. New Haven, CT: Yale University Press, 2018.

Clint Watts, *Messing with the Enemy: Surviving in a Social Media World of Hackers, Terrorists, Russians, and Fake News*. New York: Harper Paperbacks, 2019.

Internet Sources

Joe Andrews, "Fake News Is Real—A.I. Is Going to Make It Much Worse," CNBC, July 12, 2019. www.cnbc.com.

Jane E. Brody, "Are G.M.O. Foods Safe?," *New York Times*, April 23, 2018. www.nytimes.com.

Elizabeth Schulze, "Facebook, Google and Twitter Need to Do More to Tackle Fake News, EU Says," CNBC, June 14, 2019. www.cnbc.com.

Laura Spinney, "Fighting Ebola Is Hard. In Congo, Fake News Makes It Harder," *Science*, January 14, 2019. www.sciencemag.org.

Dorothy Wickenden, "How Facebook Continues to Spread Fake News," *New Yorker*, November 7, 2019. www.newyorker.com.

Cover: Fab_1